IRV SEGAL

FATAL FLAW

IN THE

TENTH

COMMANDMENT

A Jake Cooper Novel

Dedication

To my biggest fan, Cathy.
Thanks for your enthusiasm and encouragement.

Glossary

This story includes Hebrew and *Yiddish* words and phrases. I've tried to make their meaning obvious from the context. However, you may want to visit shop.irvsegal.com and request my free bonus content. It includes an audiobook with pronunciations and an ebook with a glossary of these terms I think you'll find helpful and an extra "something" I think you'll enjoy reading.

– Irv Segal

About The Author

Irv Segal graduated from *yeshiva*– Rabbinical College with a B.A. in Talmudic law and led an Ultra-Orthodox Jewish lifestyle as a young adult.

He earned a certification in computer programming and held a variety of positions in the software field before starting his own software services firm.

Irv's Jake Cooper Novels are inspired by his experiences living in an Ultra-Orthodox Jewish community.

Table of Contents

Chapter One

Chicago, IL USA 2023

Jake Cooper heard the late September downpour bouncing off the roof of his old green Chevy Nova. He struggled to see the road as the wipers thumped tirelessly in a futile effort to clear the windshield.

He navigated the Nova southbound on Western toward the Jewish cemetery where Mort would be buried.

"It's time to trade in this relic," Pinky insisted.

Jake's longtime friend, Pinky Greenberg, pitched the same request every time he rode in the old Nova. Jake could easily afford a new car, but he prudently invested his share of the lottery money he and Pinky won nearly thirty years earlier instead of blowing it on lifestyle upgrades.

The one purchase he *did* splurge on turned out to be a bust—*so far*.

Despite Pinky's prodding, Jake opted to stick with his old Nova. He patched the hole in the floor, fixed the rust spots, repaired the air conditioner, and splurged for a paint job.

Pinky invested his share of their winnings in

different ways—a new house and fancy cars. He also hired a private investigator to locate his children after his ex-wife kidnapped them when they were young. He now enjoyed a great relationship with them, and his grandchildren.

Unfortunately, all the money in the world would never bring back Jake's little Debra. She drowned when he took her boating. She was so little and innocent. He never forgave himself for his cowardice that day when his fear of the water paralyzed him.

Overcoming fears was not one of Jake's strengths.

Ask him about a Jewish legal matter and he sprang to life quoting the relevant Talmudic passages in a flash. Living an Ultra-Orthodox lifestyle and graduating from Rabbinical College as a Talmudic scholar served him well even after leaving that extreme lifestyle.

But he instantly shut down when confronted with fear.

Nearly thirty years ago one of those fears almost cost him the woman who became the love of his life. He was already quite fond of Mindy Bloom when she asked him for help during an ugly custody fight.

He was happy to answer her legal questions and advise her. But when she was accused of murdering her estranged husband he wanted to walk away.

Getting involved meant facing conflict– something he worked hard to avoid.

But Pinky shamed him into mustering the courage to get involved and prove Mindy's innocence.

Over the years their fondness blossomed into a deep love.

He thought their feelings were mutual and invested a hefty chunk of his lottery money into a diamond fit for a queen.

She didn't reject *him*, but on more than one occasion she adamantly rejected the idea of getting married, without any explanation.

Jake was patient and persistent. Every few years he knelt to ask again. But her response never waivered– until yesterday when he tried again.

This proposal resulted in Mindy saying she never wanted to see him again.

As she stormed off, Jake got the call about Mort's passing. Mindy was long gone by the time Mort's death sunk in.

He called her repeatedly with no response.

He needed her now more than ever.

Mort's death hit him hard.

Mort was the retired detective who coached Jake to

become the community's investigator and prove Mindy's innocence.

But Mort was more than just a mentor. He was one of Jake's closest friends. Besides teaching Jake to think like an investigator Mort always encouraged him and expressed how proud he was of him– something Jake's father never did.

The man who filled that void, and was responsible for having the chance to love Mindy was gone, and now it seemed that she was too.

He looked over and watched Pinky crank the passenger window open after raising his leg to release his personal *essence*.

As much as he loved his crude best friend, he couldn't help wishing Mindy was sitting there now.

He desperately wanted to reach across the seat and hold her hand.

He really needed that now.

The driving sheets of rain made it difficult to spot the entrance, but Jake caught a glimpse of the cemetery's crumbling stone wall, and entered through an open iron gate.

He maneuvered the Nova along muddy rut-laden dirt roads to the gravesite as Pinky read the directions aloud from the little printed card handed out at the *Chesed Shel Emes* funeral home.

When Pinky yelled, "Stop, this is it!" Jake parked the Nova alongside the retaining wall across from the graves.

The two mourners popped their black oversized umbrellas open, and strode across the muddy grass searching for the gravesite.

The earthy smell of drenched tree bark permeated the air.

Jake's black leather Oxford shoes sank deep into the wet ground with each step emerging with clumps of mud glued to his heels and soles.

He spotted a large mound of earth atop a plywood sheet, and noted the shovel thrust deep into the pile waiting to be extracted to cover the coffin.

They were the first to arrive.

The rain slowed.

Jake felt like the pitter patter hitting his umbrella were God's tears rejoicing in the return of an angel while empathizing with those left behind in pain.

No longer occupied with locating the gravesite, his mind was free to think about his devastating loss.

The deep pain in his heart returned.

He turned to say something to Mindy only to remember she might never again be at his side.

They had become inseparable.

He felt like a limb was missing without her next to him.

The director of the *Chesed Shel Emes* arranged for eight men to meet them at the gravesite so the traditional *Kaddish* prayer for the dead could be recited which requires a quorum of ten Jewish adult males.

The *Kaddish* needs to be recited by someone who lost a close family member.

Pinky still had his entire family.

Technically, Jake could recite it for his little Debra. But the pain that memory would surface was more than he could bear.

The funeral home director told Jake they paid followers of the *Sopoynik Rebbe–Sopoynik Chassidim*, to attend funerals, *shiva* houses, and other religious events when a quorum was needed. He assured Jake one of the eight men would qualify to recite the *Kaddish*.

The hearse arrived a few minutes later, followed by eight young men who piled out of a gray van with *Sopoynik Mitzvah Van* stenciled on the side in black.

One bearded man in his mid-thirties wearing a black

fedora approached Jake with an outstretched hand, and offered his condolences.

"I'm Benny Chinsky," he said. "My mom passed away, so I'll be the one to recite the *Kaddish*."

Jake noticed Benny's cauliflower ear, but forced himself to look straight into his deep-set eyes half covered by overgrown bushy black eyebrows.

He turned to introduce Benny to Pinky whose gaze was rudely fixated on Benny's deformity.

"Howdya get that?" Pinky inquired while motioning toward his own ear.

"Oh, *that*?" Benny replied. "I fell off a ladder when I was a kid."

Jake threw Pinky a *What the hell is wrong with you* look, and then made his way to the hearse.

The driver opened the rear door of the hearse. Jake and Pinky each grabbed one corner of the *aron*– the plain pine casket, and slid it out. Several other men helped them carry the *aron* to rest it on the straps hovering over the open grave.

The funeral home assistant slowly lowered the *aron* into its final resting place, and removed the straps.

Jake was the first to toss a shovel of dirt onto the *aron*.

It seemed to fall in slow-motion.

He heard the clumps of soil thump as they hit the wooden casket.

He suddenly felt woozy.

He stumbled toward the grave only to be saved by Pinky's strong arm gripping him, and pulling him back to safety.

Pinky and the others took turns tossing in shovels of earth until the *aron* was fully buried.

Jake listened to Benny Chinsky slowly recite the *Kaddish*.

Benny mispronounced the guttural *cheis* and *khaf* Hebrew letters, leading Jake to assume Benny was a *Ba'al Teshuva*—someone who became Ultra-Orthodox late in life, and never attended Hebrew school.

Jake thanked Benny and the others and headed back to the Nova with Pinky. They still needed to shop at the kosher bakery and grocery which both closed early on Fridays in honor of *Shabbos*—the Sabbath, which would begin at nightfall.

Jake inserted the key into the ignition, and was about to crank the engine when his cell phone buzzed.

It was Rabbi Miklin.

Jake first met his father, Rabbi Isaac Miklin, when

he headed the Illinois Rabbinical Board. After he passed, his son assumed the post which included overseeing internal community investigations.

"Now that Mort's passed, we really need *your* help," he pleaded. "There *is* no one else."

Jake was shocked when the rabbi described the case he wanted help with.

Initially, the senior Rabbi Miklin turned only to Jake for help with investigations. Mort Wolfe coached him on some cases, and used his connections as a retired Chicago detective when needed. But Mort didn't fit in despite being Jewish. The Ultra-Orthodox community didn't trust him.

Jake showed Mort how to dress the part by wearing white dress shirts, conservative ties, dark suits, and black dress shoes. He grew a beard, perched a black fedora over the big black velvet *yarmulke* snugly adorning his head, and hung his *tzitzis* strings out of his shirt.

Jake also taught Mort to speak *Yeshivish*—Rabbinical College lingo.

Eventually, the community accepted Mort as one of their own, and revealed details to him they wouldn't dare tell the police.

That's when Jake's role with Mort reversed.

Rabbi Isaac Miklin, and then his son, turned first to *Mort* for help with investigations, and *he* occasionally helped Mort with insight into the finer points of Ultra-Orthodox Jewish laws and traditions.

Jake didn't mind *helping*. He was thrilled to be relieved of the primary burden.

But now he was being thrust back into the *primary* role, and he'd be flying solo. He'd never done that before. Mort was always there for guidance and assistance.

He wasn't ready for this.

He needed Mindy now more than ever. She always knew what to say to bolster his confidence.

But she never wanted to see him again.

The case Rabbi Miklin described was the most bizarre thing he'd ever heard, and he had no idea where to start.

Chapter Two

Despite Raizy Waxman's bad leg, she managed to keep pace alongside the short, young *Rebbetzin* leading the group of wives and daughters trailing behind the men on Saturday.

She admired the *Rebbetzin's* long blonde hair despite knowing it must be a wig. She'd been living in Ultra-Orthodox communities long enough to know that married women cover their real hair.

Before them a sea of furry *shtreimels* and black hats bobbed back and forth atop the heads of the mass of men and boys trailing behind their leader, the *Sopoynik Rebbe*. They followed the *Rebbe* to his home on Mozart after *Shabbos* morning prayers to join him for lunch.

Somewhere in that blob of furry and black hats was Raizy's son.

So far, none of the *Sopoynik Rebbe's* followers– his *Chassidim*, expressed the slightest suspicion of their secret.

The peaceful early afternoon sunshine was occasionally disrupted by a passing car of gawkers taking in the strange bunch.

They were all making their way to eat the *Shabbos*

lunch meal at the *Rebbe's tish* – the *Rebbe's* table.

When they arrived Raizy followed the women into the commercial sized kitchen while the men lingered in the oversized dining room housing a long table covered with a white tablecloth embroidered with *Shabbos* images—candlesticks, *challah* breads, wine bottles, and goblets.

Three large crystal chandeliers cast reflections off the silver pieces on the table.

At the far end of the table Raizy spotted a fringed silk cover barely hiding two large *challah* breads resting on a wooden cutting board. Next to that was a large glass salt shaker with a silver top, a bottle of wine, and a huge silver goblet etched with images of grape clusters.

Raizy watched from the kitchen doorway and noticed the *Rebbe* had his left hand curled up into his sleeve hiding his fingers from sight.

The *Rebbetzin* approached Raizy from behind, and whispered, "My husband was born with only three fingers on that hand. His father was the previous *Rebbe*. When he emigrated from the European town of *Sopoynik* his *chassidim* followed him here to Chicago. When he died my husband was just a young boy. The logical choice to succeed him was his older brother. But his father proclaimed from his deathbed that my husband's missing fingers were a sign from God that *he* should be the one to lead.

"His brother was furious, but eventually seemed to accept the situation. That's why he hides his fingers—to avoid flaunting the reason for his brother's misfortune."

When the *Rebbe* moved to sit at the head of the table the men swarmed to grab the nearest open seat.

Raizy watched intently as the *Rebbe's gabbai*—his personal assistant, decanted the wine into the large silver goblet and placed the goblet into the *Rebbe's* open right palm.

The *Rebbe* steadied the goblet with the hand hidden in his left sleeve, and raised it slightly.

The noisy crowd hushed.

The *Rebbe* sang the *Shabbos Kiddush* blessing while *shuckling*—rhythmically swaying forward and backward. The men surrounding the table fell into similar rhythmic sways, and replied *omein* in unison after he concluded.

The *Rebbe* took a sip of the wine, and handed the goblet to his *gabbai* who poured the remaining wine into the wide opening of a large silver vessel with multiple tiny spouts positioned above shot glass sized silver cups. The wine immediately flowed from the large vessel into each of the cups.

The *gabbai* handed the tiny cups one-by-one to the man next to him who reserved the first one for himself, and passed along the others.

The men stood, and headed into the kitchen to wash their hands. They lined up and took turns filling a large, antique, hammered bronze washing cup adorned with floral designs, and ritually pouring water over their right and left hands three times.

One by one they dried their hands and *shuckeled* while reciting the blessing for spiritually cleansing their hands before touching bread.

Meanwhile, some of the women hustled to collect the goblet, wine, and all the tiny silver cups from the dining room table.

Raizy stood to follow and help, but the *Rebbetzin* put her hand on Raizy's shoulder. "Sit," she said. "Let the girls do that. You're our special guest."

Raizy and her son truly *were* special guests, but she wondered if the *Rebbetzin* said that because she noticed her struggling with her bad leg, or because she knew her secret.

When the men finished washing and returned to their seats the *Rebbe* removed the fringed silk *challah* cover to reveal two huge braided loaves of *challah* bread.

The *gabbai* helped him lift the two loaves until he balanced them between his good hand and the one hidden in his sleeve.

The *Rebbe* recited the blessing for bread in a sing-song voice, and then handed the loaves to his *gabbai*.

The *gabbai* carved the *challah* breads up on a large silver tray, sprinkled salt over the carnage, and let the *Rebbe* partake before passing the tray along for each man to take a piece.

Meanwhile, the women busied themselves preparing small plates of *gefilte fish* garnished with cooked onions and a single carrot slice.

The *gabbai* enlisted two men to serve the fish which the hungry crowd quickly devoured.

They passed their plates to the end of the table along with their fish forks to be collected and removed before the meat courses were served.

Raizy knew meat and dairy needed to be separated in a kosher home, but she was surprised the first time she saw fish being kept separate as well.

The men enjoyed a main course of piping hot *cholent, kishka,* and a fresh salad, in the dining room while the women enjoyed the same at a large table in the kitchen.

Raizy enjoyed the heartwarming aroma of the food almost as much as the taste.

The *Rebbetzin* insisted Raizy sit right beside her, and made her feel like family.

They could see the *Rebbe* sitting at the far end of the dining room table.

Raizy noticed the *Rebbe* and the *Rebbetzin* exchange frequent loving looks.

She spotted her son sitting amongst the men.

He seemed to be fitting in well.

While the men filled their bellies the dining room buzzed with the loud clamor of *Yiddish* banter, laughter, and an occasional utensil clink.

The *gabbai* motioned to the crowd who reacted with hushed words followed by abrupt silence.

The *Rebbe* stood, and began to speak.

He explained that for the sake of their special guests he would speak in English instead of *Yiddish*.

He spoke about *Parshas Zachor*—the *Torah* portion that had been read aloud during morning prayers.

"God commanded us to remember how the people of *Amalek* tried to kill us after we left Egypt.

"Even today there are those who plan to harm us. We must remain vigilant to stop them before they can act."

Raizy once again spotted her son, and caught his eye.

They exchanged knowing glances.

Chapter Three

Muttle Katz skillfully finished forming a letter on the *mezuzah* scroll with his quill, then carefully rested it in its cradle.

He scratched his pockmarked face through the wisps of his sparse beard, and then scratched his head with his large, black, velvet *yarmulke*.

A moment later his phone's alarm rang.

He peered through his gold wireframe glasses to see what the device was squawking about.

It was time to close the *mikvah* after the men used it to ritually bathe during their Sunday morning hours.

Aside from his meager income as a *sofer* writing and repairing holy scrolls, he and Rose enjoyed free housing and a stipend in exchange for being the *mikvah's* caretakers. He prepared for, and cleaned up after the men in the morning, and Rose did the same for the women in the evening. The Ultra-Orthodox community used the *mikvah's* ritual rainwater bath for spiritual cleansing.

When he grabbed the *mikvah* key Rose yelled from the bedroom, "Go! Close up already! You're gonna encourage stragglers. Go *now*!"

"Okay Rose," he sheepishly replied.

She was adamant that he start on time, and be done before noon to give her plenty of time to inspect, and redo things if they weren't to her standards before the women's hours began after dark. He made sure to finish no later than eleven to avoid more grief from Rose.

He resented her more each day, but he could never muster the courage to voice his opinion, or say no. He was especially sorry he hadn't said *no* to the *Rebbe* who personally arranged his match.

He hated her, and felt like she hated him too.

He was stuck for life.

That little *mikvah* key was the only thing that gave him some sense of power—the power to open that lock in the morning, and let in the early birds, and the power to lock it and deny access to latecomers.

That key was his one tiny crumb of control.

He thought about it whenever Rose bullied him, especially in bed when her emasculating words hindered his manhood.

Eventually he came to enjoy his inability to perform because it infuriated Rose without the need for him to confront her.

Despite that joy, he was still a man with needs that

needed to be fulfilled.

Their tiny house shared a common wall with the *mikvah* whose door was on the opposite side of the brown brick structure.

Muttle hugged himself to ward off the chill as he rounded the building to the *mikvah* side under overcast skies.

The last man out passed *Muttle* as he opened the door, and entered the steamy locker room.

He scooped up the damp towels strewn about the locker room, and tossed them into a large laundry bin.

He sprayed the room with Lysol, then wheeled the squeaky cart to the laundry room while mulling over his new venture idea.

Rose was after him to make enough extra money to pay for a kitchen renovation. *If you expect me to slave over your meals, you gotta get me a nicer kitchen. And don't you dare tell me we can't afford it. Figure it out Muttle!*

He was already stretched to the limit with his time handling his *sofer* business. How much more could he do?

God forbid *she* should get a job.

Rose spent the bulk of *her* day sleeping, primping, and shopping at Old Orchard mall.

He tossed the towels into the washing machine, and

deposited just the right amount of soap, softener, and bleach, into their respective compartments.

Muttle retrieved a bucket from under the utility sink, and slowly filled it.

He mopped the *mikvah* bath area and locker room while continuing to mull over the details of his new business idea.

The humidity from the showers hung in the locker room causing his wireframe glasses to slide down his sweaty nose. He pressed them dead center with his index finger to reposition them.

His new business plan seemed perfect.

It would satisfy his needs in more than one way.

Chapter Four

After Mindy told Jake she never wanted to see him again, he was devastated. They'd grown close, shared their love, and watched her children start families of their own.

All he wanted was to grow even closer when he asked for her hand in marriage.

The one big purchase he splurged his lottery winnings on nearly thirty years ago was a diamond ring big enough to make any woman's eyes pop.

But Mindy refused his proposal.

She explained that she did love him, but the psychological damage she suffered under Sender's regime made her want to keep her independence.

She wanted to maintain their relationship, but not as a married couple.

Hoping her trauma would eventually wane he asked her again a few years later only to receive the same rejection.

But Jake never gave up.

Every few years he popped the question.

Pinky warned him that his persistence could backfire.

He was right.

Just before Mort passed, Jake proposed again—this time pulling out all the stops.

He wore a tight shirt to subtly remind Mindy he worked hard to stay in shape despite his age.

He cut his hair just the way she liked it—squared off in the back, and just long enough to part. He thought about coloring it, but decided it was better to highlight the fact that despite his age his dark blond wavy hair bore only a tiny trace of gray.

He got down on one knee, and lowered his tall torso to look up into Mindy's eyes.

He finally got a different reaction from her—but not the one he hoped for.

Instead of politely refusing him she got angry, and said she never wanted to see him again.

Despite Pinky's prophecy, Jake was shocked.

When he recounted the breakup to his long-time best friend, Pinky was kind enough not to say *I warned you*.

Jake endured many restless nights, and repeatedly pleaded with Mindy to reconsider. But eventually she said firmly, "I just don't want to be with you anymore."

His mind heard her words, but his heart never forgot

the love they shared.

He couldn't let her go.

He missed her.

He *needed* her.

"I'm going to give it one more shot," he confided to Pinky.

"*Man!* You're a glutton for punishment," Pinky said, "but I do wish you luck. You're gonna need it."

Jake strategically waited for just the right moment—*Yom Kippur eve* right before the Day of Atonement.

Traditionally, this was the time to ask those you've wronged for forgiveness.

Jake ambushed Mindy as she entered the Young Israel *synagogue* on Touhy shortly before the *Yom Kippur* services began at nightfall. "I'm sorry. *Please* forgive me," he pleaded. "I love you, and only want to make you happy."

It worked.

The iron wall between them lifted.

She looked up into his eyes. "*I'm* the one who needs *your* forgiveness," she said. "I know you were only trying to express your love. But you want to be in a marriage. I'll never be able to give you that. I pushed you away to set you free. That's why I insisted I never wanted to see you again.

But it's not true. I *do* love you and I *do* want to see you. I can't let you think you did anything bad to *me*."

Mindy let out a deep breath then slowly pleaded, "I really am sorry. Can you *ever* forgive me?"

Jake was elated *and* pissed off. He hesitated a moment too long before saying, "Of course I *forgive* you, but I don't understand how you could make that decision *for* me. If giving up on being married is what it takes to be with you, I'm fine with that. More than fine, I'm just relieved to know we *can* be together. There's no one I'd rather be with than you—married or not."

After clearing the air, Jake felt like their relationship hadn't skipped a beat.

He looked forward to spending the upcoming nine days of the *Succos* Holiday with Mindy, especially the last day referred to as *Simchas Torah*.

Like every *Shabbos*, and most Jewish holidays, Ultra-Orthodox Jews don't drive on the *Simchas Torah* Holiday. Although he strayed from many of the Ultra-Orthodox traditions he observed in his youth, Jake still refrained from driving on the days it was forbidden. So he booked a room at a West Rogers Park hotel near Mindy's apartment for the entire holiday rather than walk all the way from his Evanston home.

On Monday, he joined Mindy at her apartment for an early breakfast.

Jake held Mindy's hand as they strode to Young Israel for the *Simchas Torah* Holiday morning services,

He turned up his collar, and squashed his sunglasses.

Mindy let his hand go, gripped his arm tightly, and snuggled against his warm body.

Jake leaned over, brushed aside her curly red hair, and kissed her softly.

When they arrived, Mindy entered a side door leading to the women's section while Jake swung open one of two large oak doors leading to the men's section.

As the door creaked open Jake was greeted by the cantor's chant, and a few head-turns scoffing the latecomer.

Simchas Torah celebrates a year-long cycle of sequentially reading passages from the *Torah*– the Five Books of Moses every week until reaching the end, and starting over.

The morning began with the usual obligatory prayers, but morphed into a half-drunken sweaty celebration after the final *Torah* passage was read.

A generous donor sponsored a lavish *Kiddush* buffet of spirits, sugar-crusted *kichel*—bow tie cookies, herring, and trays of kosher polish delicacies from *Shalmoski's* restaurant.

After *Kiddush* all the *Torah* scrolls were removed from the ark, and handed to men clad in suits and ties. They danced around the sanctuary with the *Torah* scrolls, and sang traditional Hebrew celebratory songs.

Occasionally, an overheated, sweaty man handed off their *Torah* to a man standing on the sidelines awaiting their turn.

Jake was about to accept a *Torah* from one elderly man when he felt a tug on his sleeve.

He turned to see the junior Rabbi Miklin motioning him to step aside for a chat.

Jake was astounded how much the younger rabbi's stately posture, fiery eyes, and long beard resembled his father. He even wore the same Homburg, long black coat, and starched white shirt. The only differences were the lack of gray hair, and the quiet shoes. His father's clacking metal shoe taps would have prevented him from sneaking up on Jake like this.

"Have you made any progress on the case?" the rabbi inquired.

At Mort's funeral the rabbi asked Jake to discretely investigate a bizarre case that had Jake baffled. Someone snapped a nude photo of one of the community's young women and was blackmailing her father. Jake was tasked with finding out who took the photo and putting a stop to the perpetrator.

It was obvious from the photo that the woman was unaware she was being photographed. What was *not* apparent was where the photo was taken, or who took it.

The woman's father, a *Sopoynik Chassid* was being threatened.

The photo was accompanied by a note. If he didn't pay a hefty sum the photo would be published on a particular website.

Rabbi Miklin explained that the father wanted to go to the police, but the *Sopoynik Rebbe* asked him to wait for Jake's help in the hopes of avoiding the inevitable gossip if the authorities were involved.

Jake felt the pressure of being the only community member with the knowledge and skill to take the lead now that Mort was gone.

Over thirty years ago, when Jake helped clear Mindy's name after she'd been accused of killing her estranged husband, the now retired Detective Roberts had referred him to Mort.

Mort took Jake under his wing, and taught him to be

a first-rate investigator.

But that was a long time ago. The confidence he once had in his investigative skills had waned.

He wanted to call Roberts for help, but the rabbi said the *Rebbe* was adamant about keeping the police out of this.

"I found out who was behind the website mentioned in the note," Jake explained to Rabbi Miklin, "but I only got the name of the company that registered the domain—not the actual owner.

"The registrar said they'd only release the owner's name with a subpoena. But that requires enlisting retired Detective Roberts to help."

The rabbi stroked his beard slowly, and cocked his eyes upward to one side.

After a long pause the rabbi said, "If you feel Detective Roberts can be trusted and can help while keeping a lid on this, I'll trust your judgment."

A moment later another overheated man shoved a *Torah* into Jake's arms and pushed him into the dancing circle.

Jake gripped the lower handles protruding from the heavy *Torah's* two wooden rollers, and leaned it against his chest. The top of the dark blue velvet cover tickled his chin.

A silver pointer and breast plate hanging from chains roped over the top two wooden handles jangled as he danced.

Torah scrolls are wound up and tied shut with a velvet belt. Jake noticed that the belt on this *Torah* was tied around the outside of it's velvet cover instead of underneath it, indicating it had a flaw rendering it unfit to read from during services. It had only been removed from the ark today to allow the men to dance with it.

Jake approached the *gabbai*—the *synagogue's* sexton, and inquired what was wrong with it.

The *gabbai* replied, "One of the letters in the section recounting The Ten Commandments faded, so we can't use it to read from during the services and we don't have the budget to fix it."

Jake knew the prohibitive cost to commission a scribe to write a new *Torah*, and assumed the person who originally donated the *Torah* must have the money to fix it. Pointing to the donor's name written in gold thread lettering embroidered on the velvet cover he asked, "Why not ask the donor to pay for the repair?"

"He wouldn't be able to afford it, " the *gabbai* replied. "He got it from his grandfather who brought it from Europe. One of his grandchildren kept it in his basement for many years. Eventually he donated it so we could put it to use, and give it a proper home. We actively used it for several years until the letter faded."

Jake thought for a while, then offered, "I'd be honored if I could sponsor the repair."

Chapter Five

Benny Chinsky parked his weather-beaten, dark blue, box van outside his next customer's home. He popped on a flat cap to ward off the drizzle, and buttoned his peacoat before exiting to fetch his equipment from the back. While rounding the van he admired the big white lettering he'd painted-- *Shomer Security Systems*.

It wasn't the original name.

He liked the business, but the original name was a constant reminder how he *inherited* it.

Recalling his injury he absently touched his mangled ear—a permanent reminder of that drunken rage.

That night still haunted him.

He arrived home after his night shift at the mall to see the monster swinging a bat at his beloved adoptive mother.

She crumpled to the floor crying out in pain.

The monster turned toward him and wound up for a swing targeting his head.

He tried to wrestle the bat from the monster, but he failed, and took a forceful blow to his ear.

When it was over he took the monster's security

business van, and drove his adoptive mother as far away as he could.

Changing the business name at least made *that* part of it his own.

Moving from city to city meant starting over frequently. But their recent move to Chicago proved to be one of the better places they lived.

He was able to grow a clientele quickly here.

The *Sopoynik Rebbe* referred him to many customers, including this one.

He was amazed how helpful this community was, and how readily they were accepted.

Choosing to become a *Sopoynik Chassid* proved to be a very fortunate decision.

Business referrals were just one of many *perks*, as he liked to think of them.

Benny slammed the van's cargo doors shut, slung his worn leather pouch over his shoulder, and headed to the front door.

He pressed the doorbell, and waited.

Nobody responded.

He pressed it again.

Still no response.

He pulled his cell phone from his peacoat pocket,

and double-checked his Tuesday schedule.

He rapped on the door.

That resulted in a woman peering briefly through the window followed by the door swinging wide open.

Benny stepped inside.

The scent of her vanilla and rose perfume aroused him.

The woman peered outside before shutting the door.

Benny watched her bolt the door, and draw the curtain across the little window in the door. He noticed how all the windows in the home had their shades drawn.

The woman turned toward Benny revealing a tight skirt and pullover top that accentuated her shapely figure. The *babushka* loosely tied around her head allowed her silky red hair to dangle freely.

Benny's elevator eyes lingered where they shouldn't as he admired the sexy vixen before him. He flashed a knowing smirk.

She showed Benny to the motion sensor that had been peeping.

He skillfully removed the cover, and replaced the battery in record time.

He looked forward to the treat awaiting him.

Chapter Six

This new year was starting out prosperously for *Muttle* Katz. The *Sopoynik Rebbe* already referred more work his way than he could handle. If the influx of new projects kept increasing at this rate he'd have to hire an apprentice.

Muttle perused the array of work spread out on the long folding table serving as his workbench. It was only Tuesday, and he was already behind schedule.

He couldn't decide which project to tackle first until Rose yelled from the bedroom, "Make sure you do the Moskowitz *tefillin* first. I promised Shelly they'd be ready by five."

He begrudgingly obliged, and went to work on the *tefillin*.

They were hand-me-downs from Shelly's great grandfather. She wanted *Muttle* to refurbish them to look new for her son's *Bar Mitzvah*.

The old relics needed a major overhaul.

The leather straps were worn thin, tattered, and the blackening had faded.

Those would need to be replaced.

Muttle worked on the *tefillin* until they were done, then left them on his workbench.

He could hear Rose snoring from the bedroom, and was grateful for a few peaceful minutes to enjoy a quick lunch.

He stepped into their dated kitchen to fix himself a tuna sandwich.

He drained and emptied a can of albacore tuna into a soup bowl, mixed in a healthy dollop of mayonnaise and just the right amount of pickle juice before rigorously mixing it, and sandwiching it between two slices of lightly toasted Jewish rye.

He placed the sandwich on a plate, added a handful of chips, and grabbed a glass of iced tea before sitting at the wobbly kitchen table.

He gingerly placed his gold wireframe glasses next to his plate, and closed his eyes to focus on savoring every morsel as he slowly sunk his teeth into the sandwich.

Suddenly Rose appeared in the kitchen doorway.

Muttle was certain she had a special radar to know precisely when he was experiencing joy.

"What are you *doing*?" she bellowed. "Didn't I tell you to finish the *tefillin*? You better step up your pace if you're ever gonna make enough to redo this lousy kitchen."

Muttle hastily took another bite. "The *tefillin* are done," he reported.

He wolfed down the rest of his sandwich, and took a swig of iced tea.

He carefully slipped on his gold wireframe glasses, gripped the table with both palms, and begrudgingly pushed his chair away from it.

As he stood to return to work the front door rattled reminding him that he still hadn't fixed the doorbell.

Muttle peered through the little window in the door, and saw a tall, chiseled, middle-aged man holding an umbrella over his wavy, dark-blonde hair.

He opened the door letting in a chill, and the sound of drizzling rain.

The stranger introduced himself as Jake Cooper, and explained that he had a *Torah* needing repair.

Muttle motioned toward his workbench, "I'm pretty backed up right now. Can it wait a few weeks?"

"I'd like to get this done quickly," Jake said. "Name your price."

Muttle felt like God was raining money on him. That gave him the confidence to quote a ridiculously exorbitant price.

He was stunned when Jake replied, "Deal! Can we

start right now?"

Muttle helped Jake extract the *Torah* from the back seat of an old Chevy Nova that seemed to have been restored to showroom condition.

Muttle took the *Torah*, carried it inside, and carefully laid it on his workbench.

He removed the silver pointer and breastplate, then untied the belt fastened outside the velvet cover.

He instructed Jake to press down on the bottom handles to slightly raise the front of the *Torah* while he slipped off the cover from the top.

Muttle came around the table, and rolled the scroll open by slowly rotating the bottom handles in opposite directions.

"Where exactly is the damage?" *Muttle* inquired.

"There's a faded letter in the tenth commandment," Jake replied. "In the second repetition."

"Oh. Okay. That's almost at the end," *Muttle* said. "You'll have to help me roll it to the part that needs work."

Torah scrolls are wrapped around two wooden rollers like an old roll of film.

Muttle cleared the surrounding area on his workbench to give them plenty of room to roll the *Torah* scroll to expose the desired passage.

The *Torah* is written in Hebrew which reads from right to left, making the passage they needed toward the end of the left side.

"Grab the left handles loosely while I wind it up from the right," *Muttle* instructed.

Muttle gripped the right handles tightly, and pulled. Jake felt his handles rotate rapidly through his loose grip. *Muttle* then rolled his side forward toward Jake, then once again gripped the handles firmly, and pulled.

Muttle repeated the process rapidly dozens of times. When the scroll neared the end of the left side *Muttle* slowed his pace, and examined the text until he finally exclaimed, "Here it is!"

They circled around to read the text from the front.

Muttle took the silver pointer, and guided it slightly above the letters mumbling to himself as he read the text looking for the flaw.

"I see the problem. Look here," he said while motioning with the pointer. "See where it says *don't covet your neighbor's wife*? The letter *Shin* is badly faded."

"How long will it take to fix it?" Jake asked.

"I'll start on it now. Come back after five. I'll have it ready for you then," *Muttle* assured him.

"Excellent," Jake replied. "Oh—can you also check

the top right handle? It seems a little loose."

"Sure," *Muttle* said.

Muttle slipped carbon paper under the top page of a pad of receipts imprinted with his name and phone number. He recorded the receipt of the *Torah*, signed and dated it, then tore off the top copy, and handed it to Jake.

The moment Jake left *Muttle* went to work.

He began by wiggling the handle that Jake said felt loose.

Jake was right—it was *loose.*

The wooden rollers were usually one solid piece including the protruding handles.

He didn't understand how the handle could be loose.

He wiggled it a little more, and started twisting it when he noticed something even more curious.

There were threads carved into the wooden roller.

He'd never seen anything like this.

He skillfully removed the parchment from the wooden roller, and jiggled it until he'd unscrewed the handle, and completely removed it.

He peered deep inside the cavity and saw the end of a little black string. He grabbed a pair of tweezers, and tugged until a small black pouch emerged.

He gingerly laid the pouch on the workbench, and gently pulled the drawstrings open.

Rose appeared seemingly out of nowhere, now perched over his back. "Whaddya got *there*?" she demanded.

Before he could respond, she snatched the pouch from the table, and peered inside.

"*Ohhh…*" she exclaimed.

Chapter Seven

Jake returned to pick up the *Torah* at just past five-thirty.

The late afternoon's light showers had now burst into a heavy downpour.

He reached back into the rear of the Nova, and fished out a blue golf umbrella from the floor. He held it outside the open car door, and extended it before stepping outside beneath it.

The rain bounced off his portable roof as he sidestepped puddles, and made his way to *Muttle's* front door.

He squashed the doorbell several times with no result. He rapped on the little window in the front door. That got *Muttle's* attention before.

Still, no one arrived.

Jake twirled around to see if anyone was nearby.

He caught a glimpse of the neighboring KFC through a break in the retaining wall where he spotted a middle-aged unshaven man wearing an oversized blue and white knitted *yarmulke* sitting on a webbed folding chair next to the garbage bin holding an umbrella. He seemed to be entertaining himself by watching the herd of cars inch their way through the drive through. He waved to each passing patron like the official KFC greeter.

Rumbling thunder followed a flash of lightning rattling the little glass pane in *Muttle's* front door. That reminded him that *Muttle* handed him a receipt earlier before he left.

He slipped the receipt out of his pants pocket, and called *Muttle's* cell. *Hello. You've reached the voice mailbox of Muttle the Sofer. Leave a message and I'll get right back to you.*

Jake left a message saying that since no one came to the door he would be back in the morning to get the *Torah*.

He returned to the Nova, and slid into the driver's seat while holding the umbrella outside the door. He collapsed it, and tossed it back onto the rear floor.

He headed north on McCormick Blvd. to his Evanston home.

Jake used his share of the lottery winnings to buy a three-bedroom, split-level, fixer upper on a quiet, tree-lined, dead-end street. It didn't have a garage, but unlike his old apartment in the city there was plenty of open street parking, and a driveway.

The pelting rain still hadn't let up.

He pulled up the driveway, and inched as close as he could to the tiny, covered front porch.

He grabbed the umbrella, leaped from the Nova onto the covered porch, and unlocked the front door.

Standing in the tiny entrance he opened the umbrella, held it outside the open door, and twirled it to shake off the rainwater. He partially collapsed it, and propped it up in the corner on the weatherproof mat inside the door to finish drip drying.

Jake slipped off his shoes, and sunk his feet into the blue, cozy slippers waiting for him near the door. Two additional pairs remained, each a different size and color. The small pink set was for Mindy, and the big brown ones were for Pinky. He originally thought about buying the *pink* set for Pinky, but then decided against it. Teasing him about his name occasionally was one thing. Rubbing it in his face every time he visited would be over the top.

He instituted the slipper mandate after refinishing the wood floors, and laying white carpeting in the living room.

He climbed a short staircase up one level, and headed to the front bedroom which he used as a home office. He tossed his wallet and keys into a brown leather tray on top of the antique desk situated next to a full-sized globe.

He checked his cell phone to see if *Muttle* had responded.

There were no messages.

Jake climbed back down two levels to the home's lower level.

He stretched out on one of the two black-leather reclining sofas he used to form an L-shape, clicked the remote to watch reruns of Magnum, and plopped his cell onto the white coffee table.

It wasn't long before the sounds of the storm lulled him into a deep sleep.

He slept late into the morning until the incessant ringtone of his cell woke him.

"Oh, hi rabbi. I haven't made any more progress with the photo issue," Jake said preemptively.

"Thanks for the update, but I'm calling to ask for your help with another matter entirely—a time-sensitive matter," Rabbi Miklin replied. "Can you stop by my office right away?"

"Okay, sure." Jake said. "But first I need to pick up a *Torah* that *Muttle* Katz is fixing for me."

Silence.

"*Rabbi*? You still there?"

"Yes," the rabbi replied. "But *Muttle* Katz won't be able to help you."

"*What*? Why not?" Jake asked.

"*Muttle* Katz is the reason I'm calling," the rabbi explained. "He's dead. Please come directly to my office. I'll explain when you get here."

Jake splashed some water on his stubbled face, and fetched his keys and wallet from the upstairs office.

As he rushed out the front door the sight of Pinky's slippers reminded him they were meeting at Blind Faith Cafe for breakfast.

He called Pinky, and rescheduled for lunch.

Jake cranked up the Nova, and headed to Rabbi Miklin's office.

He swung the outside door open letting in a gust of wind that threatened to scatter the stack of flyers on the receptionist's desk. A few pages sailed before she slammed her hands down to secure the remainder of the stack.

"Hi Jake," she said. "Pull that door shut tight so the wind doesn't fling it open. Rabbi Miklin's waiting for you," she added, nodding toward the corridor.

Jake noted how little the place had changed over the years.

The old orange and chrome couch had been

reupholstered with sleek black leather, and the elderly receptionist had been replaced with a younger one. The rest was exactly how he remembered it the first time he visited Rabbi Miklin's father all those years ago.

As he made his way down the tiled hallway he swore he could hear the taps of the elder rabbi's shoes. A chill shot up the back of Jake's neck when he saw the younger Rabbi Miklin standing in his office doorway waiting to greet him. He looked exactly like his father—the same tall stately stance, Homburg, long black coat, and stark white shirt, minus the wrinkles and white hair.

The rabbi waved Jake into his office and toward the guest chair. He gently closed the door before nestling himself into his own worn, brown, leather executive chair.

Jake was eager for details, but he knew the rabbi well enough to be patient.

Rabbi Miklin leaned forward resting his elbows on his old wooden desk causing the wood to creak. He slowly pressed his fingertips together forming a steeple, and then repeatedly separated and pressed them together as if trying to think of the right words to say.

Despite his urge to prod the rabbi along, Jake held his tongue.

Finally, the rabbi said, "As I said, *Muttle* is dead.

His body was found in the *mikvah*. It *looks like* he drowned himself—like *suicide*. His wife, Rose, knows the shame and embarrassment suicide will bring on her. She insists *Muttle* was not suicidal. She called the *Sopoynik Rebbetzin* asking her for help who immediately had her husband call me to see if I could get you to investigate. I'm hoping you'll take this on right away so Rose can at least tell the community the matter is being investigated before everyone assumes it was suicide."

"Did he leave a note or tell someone he intended to kill himself?" Jake asked.

"No," the rabbi replied.

"Well, then it's not technically suicide according to *Halachah*," Jake said.

"That's true," the rabbi replied. "But even though the circumstances don't fit the Jewish *legal* definition of suicide, that won't stop the community rumor mill."

The rabbi pressed his palms flat onto the desk and leaned forward. "Please say yes so I can tell the *Sopoynik Rebbe* you're taking the case. He'll spread the word quickly to quash the rumors before they get out of hand."

Jake knew exactly how quickly the *yenta* machine fired up, and the damage it could do.

"Of course," Jake assured him. "I'll start today."

"Excellent!" the rabbi responded. "You should get to the *mikvah* right away to get a look at things before the police seal it off. That's where Rose found him—drowned in the *mikvah*. She hasn't called the police yet—she's waiting for your help."

Jake was miffed the rabbi assumed he would take the case before speaking with him, but he knew he had to step up.

Jake arrived to see Rose just before noon. He rang the bell, and knocked on the little window in the door.

After a few rounds of ringing and window rattling he rounded the building, and tapped on the *mikvah* door.

The door flew open almost immediately revealing a woman dressed sexier than Jake expected.

"Jake Cooper?" she asked.

"Ya," he replied. "Rose?"

She nodded.

She let Jake in, and locked the door behind her.

"Rabbi Miklin asked me to rush over," Jake said. "I'm so sorry to hear about *Muttle*. I was just here yesterday dropping off a *Torah*. He seemed fine. What happened?"

"I really don't know, but I know he wouldn't do this on purpose. He's over here," she said while motioning Jake to follow her.

They entered the locker room, and passed a large laundry cart overflowing with wet towels.

The moment they entered the *mikvah* chamber the hot steam sent salty sweat running down Jake's forehead, and into his eyes.

The first thing he noticed was the worn leather soles of *Muttle's* black shoes starkly offset by his white socks.

Jake peered into the tiny, tiled rainwater pool, and saw the same scraggly beard and pockmarked face he met yesterday. *Muttle's* gold wireframe glasses were still perched on his nose.

One of the lenses was shattered.

Rose collapsed, and let out a long cry of grief as if she had stumbled upon the body for the first time.

Ultra-Orthodox Jewish rules forbid men from touching women they aren't married to, so Jake comforted her with words rather than a hug. "I'm so sorry," he said.

Rose continued weeping.

Jake couldn't help but notice her full chest squeezed into a body-tight sweater heaving as she gasped for air between sobs.

Suddenly, it occurred to him that she locked the door after letting him in. The two of them were alone—also a big Ultra-Orthodox no-no. He assumed she wasn't thinking straight, given the shock she was dealing with.

He waited for her cries to subside into soft whimpers before asking, "What makes you think this looks like suicide? If he was trying to drown himself, he'd probably be face down in the water—not on his back."

"He was," Rose explained. "I turned him over to see who it was. It took a moment to sink in when I saw. I couldn't believe it. I still can't believe it."

Jake *the investigator* wanted to say she shouldn't have touched the body. But Jake *the man* knew that's not something she needed to hear *now*.

"Tell me *exactly* what happened," Jake instructed, "from the time you last saw *Muttle* until you found him."

Rose took a moment, then replied, "I'd already gone to bed. *Muttle* came to bed later after he finished his projects for the day. I slept in—"

Jake interrupted her, "Just to confirm, we're talking about last night, right?"

"Yes," she said, "last night. I slept in late this morning. *Muttle* wasn't home when I got up. I assumed he went to open the *mikvah* for the men. I got busy getting breakfast ready. When he still hadn't returned, I called his cell. His voicemail picked up, which was weird. He *always* answers when he knows it's *me* calling."

Rose seemed to drift into a trance. Her head tilted. Her eyes wandered as if searching for something.

"What did you do after that?" Jake prodded.

After a long pause Rose took a deep breath, and slowly exhaled.

"I went to the *mikvah* parking lot. I couldn't go inside during the men's hours, but I hoped to catch one of them entering or leaving the *mikvah*. Eventually, a man arrived, and I asked him to go inside to tell *Muttle* to come out to meet me. But when he tried to pull the door open it was locked. After he left, I used *my* key to open the door and—well, you know the rest."

"I know this is hard for you, and it doesn't seem like much now," Jake said, "but it *will* help me figure out what really happened."

Jake called retired Detective Roberts, and explained the situation. After chewing out Jake for trampling the scene Roberts assured him that someone from the Rogers Park District would be there within the hour.

It was already time to meet Pinky.

Jake knew how Pinky got when he wasn't fed on time, and didn't want to push it to a late lunch. He instructed Rose to wait for the police to arrive, and told her not to touch anything more.

"Just tell them exactly what you told me, and let them do their thing. Meanwhile, I'll start my own investigation."

Chapter Eight

On Wednesday, Jake drove to meet Pinky for lunch at Blind Faith.

He squinted periodically as intense sun rays flashed between white cloud puffs while guiding the Nova east on Dempster.

He cranked the window open hoping the crisp air would help him get clarity on what was bothering him about *Muttle's* death and Rose's behavior. He looked forward to picking Pinky's brain, who occasionally shed light where he couldn't. A good carrot juice dose often sparked Pinky's inspiration.

Jake entered the vegetarian café, and scanned the long line looking for his tall muscular friend, hoping to spot his head of curly blond hair.

"Jake! Over here!" Pinky said, waving at Jake to join him near the front of the line.

Jake made his way to Pinky earning questioning looks as he passed people in line.

He joined his hungry friend standing behind a middle-aged, tattooed couple wearing matching snakeskin boots, stonewashed jeans, and black Harley tank tops.

Staring at the two pony tails hanging before them Jake asked, "When did you get here? I thought I was on time. You must *really* be famished!"

He waited to reveal anything about the morning's events until they were seated.

Just as he brought Pinky up to speed, a waitress appeared to take their drink orders.

"I think you need two large carrot juices for yourself," Jake suggested. "I really need your thinking cap at full capacity."

While waiting for their drinks they perused the menu, and took in the aroma of fresh meals emanating from passing trays.

After settling on a Blind Faith Burger Jake said, "There's so many things bothering me about this I'm not sure where to begin."

The waitress returned with their drinks.

Pinky took a long draw through the carrot juice straw. "Well, why not just start at the start! What's the first thing that bothered you?"

Amazed at the orange brain nectar's immediate jump start, Jake replied, "I knew I could count on you."

Jake thought for a moment, then said, "I suppose the first thing was why nobody answered the door when I came to get the *Torah* yesterday. *Muttle* told me to get it anytime after five, and assured me it would be ready. That seemed odd. And when *Muttle* turned up dead today—well, that just seemed *too* coincidental. On top of that, Rose specifically told me *Muttle had* finished my *Torah*. So why *wasn't* he there when he said he *would* be?"

Pinky squirmed in his seat, wrestled a pen from his pants pocket, and held it up. "Here you go Sherlock," he said as he slapped it on a napkin, and slid it across the table. "Start a list, and let's see if we can make sense of anything."

Pinky nursed his carrot juice while Jake started writing.

"What else ya got?" Pinky asked.

"Well, his glasses," Jake said. "If he drowned himself on purpose, why would his eyeglass lens be smashed? Why would he even be *wearing* them? Wouldn't he take them off before going under the water? And if he was pushed, or slipped face forward, it's more likely *both* lenses would be smashed. But only one was."

"Maybe he *was* pushed or slipped but hit the corner of something that only smashed one lens," Pinky suggested.

"That's what *I* thought," Jake agreed. "But I didn't see anything around the *mikvah* in his path with corners or edges that would only catch one lens."

They sat silently for a few moments.

Pinky removed the straw from his carrot juice, and tossed back the tumbler to extract the last drop. He slowly lowered the glass to the table, and raised a finger with his free hand. "Unless…," he said.

"Unless what?" Jake demanded.

"Unless that lens was already smashed *before* he fell into the *mikvah*."

Chapter Nine

Jake waited to hear from Roberts Thursday afternoon.

He finally called just after noon. "They're done with the scene. Word is it'll be ruled an an accidental death—not suicide."

"Rose will be relieved," Jake replied. "I agree it's unlikely that it was *suicide*. But I'm not convinced it was an accident."

"You think he was *murdered*?" Roberts asked.

"I don't know," Jake admitted. "But I think there's more to it—something's *off* about the whole thing."

Now that the police released the scene, Jake decided to return to *Muttle's* home to retrieve the *Torah*.

Jake's trench coat and umbrella were no match for the driving rain and strong wind. He was soaked despite the short hop from the Nova to the front door.

Rose opened the door after one round of knocking.

Most of her red hair was trapped under a black *babushka*, but a few wisps managed to escape. Despite her black, long-sleeved top and ankle length skirt, Jake thought she looked a little too sexy for a wife mourning her husband.

She let Jake in, and locked the door, leaving the two of them alone.

While shaking off the rain, and resting his folded umbrella by the door he noticed the large mirror above the mantle covered with a white sheet, and the couch cushions leaning against the wall-- both customary at a *shiva* house. The mirrors are covered so you think about the deceased instead of yourself. The removal of the cushions force mourners to sit low to the ground as an expression of grief.

"I was hoping to get the *Torah Muttle* fixed for me," Jake said as he caught a whiff of vanilla.

"Oh," Rose replied, sounding a bit disappointed. "Sure. It's still on his workbench."

As Jake followed her to the *Torah* he asked, "Has anything else come to mind that you didn't tell me before?"

Rose spun around abruptly, and scrunched her forehead. "Are you implying I'm *hiding* something?" she growled.

"Of course not!" Jake assured her, even though he *was* fishing for something specific. "Not at all. Just that you musta been in shock before, so maybe you remembered something since then."

"No. Nothing," she replied in a calmer tone.

Jake decided to lay it out for her.

"*Muttle* told me to pick up the *Torah* any time after five the day before you found him. I was here at five-thirty, but no one answered the door. Where were you guys?"

"How should *I* know?" she said. "I was out shopping at Old Orchard."

"Okay," Jake said, motioning her to calm down. "I'm not *accusing* you of anything, just trying to make sense of it. When you got back, where was *Muttle*?"

Rose took a long deep breath. "Come to think of it, I didn't see him. But I was running late, and rushing to get the *mikvah* ready for the women. I only saw him later that night when he came to bed."

She pointed to a *Torah* laying on *Muttle's* workbench. "That's it," she said.

Jake walked around the table to lift the *Torah* by its bottom handles. As he approached the edge of the workbench he felt his foot kick something. He peered under the table, and located an old eyeglass pouch with a clip. He lifted it, and handed it to Rose. "*Muttle* must have dropped this."

Rose examined the case. "These aren't *Muttle's*," she said while extracting a pair of coke bottle glasses.

"Maybe they belong to a customer that dropped

them," Jake suggested. "Mind if I take them? I have an idea how to get them back to their rightful owner."

Jake pocketed the glasses, wrapped his trench coat around the *Torah*, and carried it to the Nova.

While laying the *Torah* on the rear seat he felt the top right handle wiggle. *Muttle was supposed to fix that.*

Now it seemed even looser than before.

Chapter Ten

Early *Shabbos* afternoon Jake found himself longing for Mindy's company. He'd not only fallen in love with *her*, but also with the scrumptious Friday night and Saturday *Shabbos* meals they enjoyed together.

He *thought* their relationship was okay after Mindy explained *why* she refused to marry him, and he agreed to let that go to be with her.

But he still had the ring. It was just sitting there in his bedside drawer.

Earlier that week, he got the bright idea to wrap it, and give it to her—not as a marriage proposal, but as a gift.

But when she unwrapped it the excitement in her eyes turned to anger. She threw it at him. "How could you! After all we went through. You said you understood. But you don't. You just don't get it."

No matter how much Jake emphasized it was just a gift she wasn't having it.

She insisted he leave, and told him not to bother coming for *Shabbos*.

He hoped she would have calmed down, and made up before *Shabbos*.

But that didn't happen.

How could Mindy just shut off the feelings he knew she still had for him?

He knew *he* couldn't.

Driving on *Shabbos* was prohibited so Jake took advantage of the crisp sunny weather, and walked to West Roger's Park where Mindy still lived. They used to walk off *Shabbos* lunch together by strolling through Indian Boundary Park, so that's where he headed in hope of catching her there.

He followed the North Shore Channel Trail south enjoying the white noise *whoosh* of McCormick Boulevard traffic while dodging the occasional jogger or biker.

Jake entertained himself on the long journey thinking about how he was going to find out who owned those eyeglasses. He suspected they would know something about *Muttle's* death, or at the very least could pinpoint his whereabouts at a given time.

The eyeglass case was embossed with the name of the Optometrist. Given the unusually thick lenses he reasoned that it should be easy for them to search their files for the name of the patient. He wasn't sure if HIPAA laws would be a problem. He might need Roberts to help but figured he'd take it one step at a time.

It was late afternoon by the time he arrived at the park. He stopped just to rest for a minute on the first bench he encountered, but he fell into a deep sleep. The crisp air, sunshine, and exercise had taken their toll.

"*Jake*? Jake! Are you okay?" a voice yelled.

After realizing he wasn't dreaming, he opened his eyes, and saw grass and dirt through the old bench's wooden slats. He felt the grip of a hand shaking his shoulder.

"Thank God! I thought you were dead!"

He recognized the voice as the one he longed to hear.

He pushed himself up to meet Mindy's eyes. He could see the love reflecting his.

"Oh, hi Mindy. No—not dead, just *dead-tired* I guess."

"Why are you *here*?" she asked.

"I walked from Evanston," Jake explained. "It's such a nice day so—"

"You walked *here*? You could've just walked to Central Park in Skokie. That's much closer to you," she said. "Why are you *really* here?"

"I just don't understand what happened. All I did was try to give you a nice gift. I know you love me. I see it in your eyes."

"Of course I love you," Mindy said. "I couldn't stop loving you even if I wanted to."

"So why did you do that to us again? Why did you shut me out? I really need to know," Jake pleaded. "What did I do wrong *this* time?"

"I'm sorry. I know you meant well, but that ring just triggers something in me," she replied. "You know—the whole marriage thing."

"I get that," Jake said, "but I just wanted you to have it as a gift."

"Even as a gift it bothers me," Mindy replied. "I know it makes no sense. Can you forgive me?"

Jake stood and took her hands in his. "Of course I do."

"So, are we good?" Mindy asked.

"Yes," Jake said, "but I wish you'd tell me how you feel when it happens. I've spent the last few days torturing myself trying to figure out what I did wrong."

He pulled her close, looked deeply into her eyes, and softly kissed her forehead.

Mindy took Jake's hand, turned around, and tugged him forward. "Come on mister. Let me make it up to you with a nice *shaleshudes* meal."

The third *Shabbos* meal— *shaleshudes* was usually Jake's least favorite *Shabbos* meal. But Mindy had a way of turning it into a culinary treat.

They walked the few blocks to Mindy's apartment on Lunt, hand-in-hand.

Jake sat at the tiny kitchen table sipping a tall glass of iced tea watching Mindy work her magic.

While she busied herself, Jake brought her up to speed on *Muttle's* death investigation.

"The Optometrist's name and address is embossed on the case, and the thick lenses are pretty unique," Jake said. "I'm planning to go there to see if they can tell me who has that exact prescription."

"What 's the Optometrist's name?" Mindy asked.

"I think it was Eisenman, or Eisen-something " Jake said.

"Eisen*stein*?" Mindy asked. "*Freddy* Eisenstein?"

"Yes—that's it," Jake said. "You *know* him?"

"Sort of," Mindy said while sliding a small cookie sheet out of the fridge.

When she laid it on the kitchen table Jake could see it had a pre-baked flat layer of dough.

"I used to take Adam there for his glasses," she explained, referring to her oldest son who was now grown with kids of his own.

"A lot of the Ultra-Orthodox crowd go to him. He's a *Sopoynik Chassid*. Actually he's the *rebbe's gabbai*."

Jake watched Mindy glaze the crust with lemon pie filling, then meticulously organize fruit into rows of contrasting colors. She began with a row of blueberries along one edge followed by a row of banana slices, and followed that with a row of kiwi slices. She repeated the pattern until the crust was completely covered with colorful rows of fruit.

It was a work of art.

She started cutting it into squares, and gently laying them out on a serving platter.

There was a loud knock on her front door.

"You expecting someone?" Jake asked.

"No," She said, giving Jake a puzzled look.

He followed her to the front door.

She peered through the peephole, then slid the security chain open, and swung the door wide to greet her tall lanky unshaven visitor.

"Hi Harold! Good *Shabbos*. Come on in. It's so good to see you."

Jake's nose twitched in response to the pungent odor that filled the entire living room the moment Harold stepped inside.

"Harold, this is my—this is Jake Cooper."

Jake offered his hand while sizing up Harold.

There was something familiar about him.

An oversized blue and white knitted *yarmulke* was perched on his head. His gray wool suit looked like it shrunk in the wash. The open collar of his yellowed, white dress shirt revealed sweat stains around the neck. The yellowed cuffs were exposed by the shrunken suit jacket sleeves. An old Lord Elgin watch peered out from beneath the left sleeve. His dirty, white socks screamed out between his untied black wingtips, and his shrunken trouser legs.

Jake pulled Mindy aside. "Can we talk privately for a minute?"

Mindy gave Jake a puzzled look, then said to Harold, "Make yourself comfortable on the couch. I'll get us some refreshments."

She followed Jake back to the kitchen.

One of the things he wanted to ask her was why she didn't introduce him as her boyfriend, but that would have to wait."

"Who is this guy?"

"Harold's parents were close with my parents," Mindy explained. "They used to visit each other nearly every *Shabbos* afternoon. His parents were murdered by terrorists shortly after they moved to Israel."

Jake shook his head. "That's awful," he said.

"Harold *was* a brilliant attorney—made partner at his firm," Mindy continued. "But he snapped after they were killed."

"When did that happen?" Jake asked.

"It was a long time ago, but he still lives in his parent's old house. Most of the time he just wanders the streets."

Mindy set the kitchen table with the fruit tart, and a tall pitcher of iced tea.

She fetched Harold from the living room, and they all sat in the kitchen for *shaleshudes*.

"Now I remember!" Jake blurted. "I *knew* you looked familiar. Didn't I see you sitting outside the KFC next to the *mikvah*?"

Mindy shot an angry stare at Jake.

"Ignore him," she said to Harold.

"No," Harold replied. "Jake is absolutely correct. That's one of my favorite places to people-watch. I see lots of fascinating people order at the drive through, and then park to eat. It's entertaining."

"Really?" Jake asked. "What's so fascinating about

that?"

"Usually it's about how different people look, and how they go about devouring their food. But sometimes it's more about *who* I see."

"Now *that* sounds interesting," Jake exclaimed. "Who are the most interesting people you've seen there?"

Mindy shot another dagger look at Jake, and shook her head.

But Harold seemed excited to share. "Oh, I've seen some local politicians, and the occasional TV personality. But I've seen several people from the community pull through there that shouldn't be eating at KFC."

Jake replied, "Well, they might just be getting a drink—there's nothing technically un-kosher about that."

"True," Harold admitted. "Still, they shouldn't be going there. Plus, I've seen some order *more* than just a drink."

"Maybe they bought food for someone else," Jake suggested, trying to defend their actions.

"Okay," Harold conceded. "But I saw one of them order chicken, and then park to eat it themselves. One of those *Sopoynik Chassidim*—that guy with the funny ear. He was driving an old blue box van with white lettering—some kind of security business."

"Benny Chinsky?" Jake asked. "You *saw* Benny Chinsky eating KFC chicken?"

"Ya—that's his name, *Benny*," Harold said. "I've seen him around town driving that van.

Chapter Eleven

Jake maneuvered the Nova into an open spot near Eisenstein Eye Care on Central in downtown Evanston.

He checked the meter to verify there was no charge to park there on Sunday.

The overcast morning sky made it hard to read the faded lettering on the wooden sign swinging above the door.

The tiny storefront was wedged between a Starbucks and an art gallery.

Jake pulled the door open, and heard a bell jingle.

A tall, muscular, middle-aged, bearded man emerged from the rear. He was wearing a large, black, velvet *yarmulke*, and his *payos*—his long curly sidelocks, were tightly wound, and tucked behind each ear. The name badge pinned to his freshly starched lab coat informed Jake this was the man he was seeking—*Dr. Fred Eisenstein, Optometrist*.

Jake introduced himself, and explained the reason for his visit.

The doctor invited Jake to sit on one of the two worn leather, swivel stools on one side of a small counter while he settled into an old, oak office chair on the other side. The doctor slid the mirror between them to one side. "HIPPA laws prevent me from disclosing patient information," he said, "but I can certainly look at the case and the glasses."

Jake heard his stool squeal as he twisted to slip the eyeglass pouch from his pants pocket. He handed it to the doctor who examined the front and back of the vintage pouch, then gently ran his thumb up and down the pocket clip.

"This is definitely one of mine, but I haven't used these in years. We use clamshell cases now."

As the doctor extracted the glasses from the pouch his furrowed brows and flaring nostrils signaled the end of his friendly demeanor.

"These are *my* glasses," he exclaimed. "I usually wear contacts, but I wear these when my eyes get tired. Where *exactly* did you say you found these?"

"I didn't," Jake replied. "Where did you lose them?"

" Look," Dr. Eisenstein growled as he placed his palms on the counter, and leaned in toward Jake. "I don't know who sent you, or what kind of stunt you're trying to pull, but I'm not telling you anything."

Jake wasn't expecting a confrontation. He felt the urge to explode at the man who suddenly rose to his number one person of interest in *Muttle's* death. But he could hear Mort whispering in his ear, *keep your cool and play this right*. His deceased mentor was still guiding him from beyond the grave.

"That's okay *Freddy*," Jake calmly replied, purposefully disrespecting the man. "These were found by *Muttle* Katz's workbench shortly after his death. I'm sure you knew *Muttle* the *Sofer*—a fellow *Sopoynik Chassid* of yours, no?"

"Who do you think you--" The doctor paused then blurted, "Wait a minute—Jake Cooper. Ya, I thought that name sounded familiar. You're that guy the *Rebbe* requested to investigate that photograph."

"Yes," Jake admitted. "I'm the guy. But I'm not here about that. How do *you* know about that?"

The doctor hesitated a second too long, then poked his finger at his chest. "I'm the *Rebbe's gabbai*. I'm his right-hand man and most trusted advisor."

Jake swiveled his chair thinking about the doctor's odd behavior, then said, "Oh, I think there's more to it than that. I think it's more *personal* for you somehow. Why *were* you at *Muttle's* place?"

"It's certainly not what you're implying," the doctor insisted. "I had nothing to do with *Muttle's* death."

"So what *were* you doing there?" Jake asked.

"I went there about that photograph," the doctor replied. "Someone dropped an envelope on the *Rebbe's* doorstep anonymously. Inside, there was that photo and a note demanding money that said *one of yours,* and threatened to post it on the Internet if he didn't pay."

"What does that have to do with *Muttle*?" Jake asked.

"The *Rebbe* doesn't have children," the doctor explained, "so he took it to mean it was a nude photograph of the daughter of one of his *chassidim.*"

"So he asked you to find out who was in the photo?" Jake asked.

"No," the doctor replied. "He didn't show the photograph to me. He just explained what it was."

"I still don't get why you were at *Muttle's*," Jake said.

"*Patience*! I'm getting to that," the doctor said. "Later that day he showed it to his *Rebbetzin.* She recognized the girl as *my* daughter—*Tzippy.*"

"Oh," Jake said. "That's awful that you had to see that."

"Yes, that was hard to look at. At first they wouldn't show it to me. But I kept pushing to see it thinking I might be able to figure out who took it. Eventually they relented, and I was right. I figured out where, how, and *who* took it."

"Oh? *How*?" Jake asked.

"The towel," he replied.

Jake cocked his head to one side. "I don't follow," he said.

"There was a towel on the floor in the photograph that had a tag on it," the doctor explained."

"How'd you figure all that out from a towel tag?" Jake asked.

"You really have zero patience," the doctor said. "I used a magnifying glass to get a closer look at the tag. I see that same tag every day when I take the *Rebbe* to the *mikvah*. Their towels have a custom label so people don't take them home. It's a black tag with big white letters that says *MIKVAH PROPERTY*."

Suddenly Jake recalled seeing a bin full of dirty towels with that label on them when he met Rose at the *mikvah* the day she found *Muttle*.

"Okay," Jake admitted. "So that means it was probably taken inside the *mikvah*. But how does that tell you who took it? Anyone at the *mikvah* can take a picture with their phone."

"The angle," the doctor replied. "Have you seen the photograph?"

"Ya, I saw it." Jake said.

"Then you know it was taken from above. If someone used their phone it would have been a very different angle. So it must have been a hidden camera in the ceiling, and you *know* who has access to the attic—it's a shared attic above the residence and the *mikvah*."

"So you assumed *Muttle* set up a camera in the attic, and used the images to make money?" Jake asked. "I didn't really know him, but he didn't strike me as someone who'd do that."

Dr. Eisenstein said, "You really can't know *what* anyone is capable of given the opportunity *and* thinking nobody would find out."

"Okay. So how did your glasses end up at *Muttle's* place?" Jake asked.

The doctor raised one brow, and cocked his eye toward the ceiling. "I must have left them after I went to pick up the *mezuzahs* I ordered for the doors on the addition to *Rebbe's* house."

A sudden jingle at the front door distracted Jake.

He swiveled to see a heavyset woman in her thirties

with a long, blonde wig starkly contrasting her black eyebrows wearing a white long sleeved top, a pleated long black skirt, and white sneakers. She held the door open to let in a tornado of twin young redheaded boys dressed alike in black pants, white socks, and black tie shoes. Their half untucked white dress shirts exposed the racing stripes of their *tzitzis*, and let the white strings dangle from the four corners. Each wore identical gold wireframe glasses. The red freckles on their little faces matched their red hair. Their large, black *yarmulkes* miraculously stayed on their heads as they raced to grab the unoccupied swivel stool. Their freshly curled, red *payos* hung like springs from both ears, and swung wildly as the two monsters took turns sitting on the stool while the other violently spun it around.

The doctor stood to greet his customer holding his hands behind his back. "Good to see you Mrs. Wolfson! Are the twins a year older already? It goes by so fast. I'll be ready for their exams in a moment. I was just finishing up with this gentleman," he said, nodding toward Jake.

The doctor shook Jake's hand. "Thanks for stopping by," he said while vigorously ushering him out the door.

That's when Jake noticed the cuts and bruises on the doctor's knuckles.

Chapter Twelve

After being rushed out of Doctor Eisenstein's shop Jake called Pinky.

"I need to finish my conversation with him," Jake responded when Pinky asked how his meeting went. "Meet me at Blind Faith—I'll fill you in."

Jake arrived a few minutes before the café opened, and waited outside for Pinky. He heard the roar of Pinky's Maserati before he saw it round the corner, then slow to a growl as he prowled for a parking spot.

The two were seated when the doors opened, and were the first and only patrons.

"Turns out the glasses I found at *Muttle's* are Dr. Eisenstein's *own* glasses. He recognized them immediately, but seemed shaken when I told him *where* I found them."

"Interesting," Pinky said. "How'd he explain *that*?"

"He said he musta accidentally left them after going there to pick up an order. But—"

Chatter from the self-service side of the eatery distracted Jake. A young man wearing a knitted *yarmulke* and a small boy in brown corduroy overalls who Jake gauged to be no older than five were placing their order at the counter. Jake listened as the man coaxed the boy to place his order. "How about those chocolate chip pancakes? You liked those last time."

"Ya!" the boy gleefully replied. "And root beer!"

The two sat at a table.

"Sorry," Jake said. "Where was I?"

"You said he left the glasses by accident, but—. What's the *but*? You're killin' me," Pinky pleaded.

"Oh ya," Jake continued. "He found out that the girl in the nude picture was his own daughter, and he placed it at the *mikvah*."

"The *mikvah*? How'd he figure that out?" Pinky asked.

"He recognized the label on a towel. The *mikvah* has distinct customized labels," Jake explained.

"Pancakes and root beer!" someone yelled from behind the counter.

Jake watched the man tell the boy to wait at the table while he went to get the food. The man returned with a large cup, and a straw. He set them on the table, and went back for the pancakes. The boy tried to insert the straw into the open cup. He couldn't quite reach high enough, and tipped the cup over.

The cup hit the floor.

The lid popped off.

Root beer splashed everywhere.

The boy stood over the disaster, tucked his hands under his brown corduroy overall straps, and hung his head like he was assessing the damage.

The man rushed back to the table. The boy conjured up a puppy dog face and said, "*I* didn't do it."

The man motioned with his hands at the empty tables surrounding them. "Then who *did*?" he asked.

With his hands still tucked under the straps the boy shrugged his shoulders, and replied, "It just *spilled*."

Pinky beckoned Jake to return to their conversation with his snapping fingers. "So? He finds out his daughter was photographed nude at the *mikvah*, and you believe he just went to *Muttle's* to pick up an order?"

"Of course not," Jake said. "Any dad woulda marched over there to confront *Muttle*. He even implied he knew *Muttle* photographed her because his residence shares the attic over the *mikvah*."

Their meals arrived, and they ate in silence.

After wolfing down their food Pinky took a long drag on his carrot juice straw. "Didn't you say one of *Muttle's* lenses was smashed—only *one*?" he asked.

"Ya—only *one*, which is odd," Jake noted.

Pinky looked up, and placed his index finger on his chin as if he were pressing his thinking cap's *on* button. "And when you showed up to get the *Torah* nobody was there even though that's when *Muttle* told you to get it, right?

"Well, I *assumed* nobody was there," Jake clarified. "Nobody answered the door, and the place looked dark."

Pinky took another hit of carrot juice. "Okay, hear me out. Maybe Eisenstein *did* go there to confront *Muttle*. And suppose that was shortly before you arrived."

"Okay," Jake said. "Where ya going with this?"

Pinky put up a hand in the *stop* position. *"Let me finish*! Maybe the good doctor couldn't contain himself, and punched *Muttle* in the eye smashing one lens. And perhaps during that altercation Eisenstein's glasses fell on the floor, and he didn't even notice. If he just *left* them there accidentally he would've left them on the *table*, not on the floor."

Jake raised a finger, and opened his mouth to blurt out a thought, but Pinky gave him the *stop* signal again.

"Let's take this one step further," Pinky continued, "maybe he hit *Muttle* so hard it killed him. Then he heard you at the door so he shut the lights until you left. Maybe *he* took *Muttle's* body, and placed it in the *mikvah* to look

89

like suicide."

Jake was dumbfounded.

"That musta been a *supercharged* carrot juice! I'll admit it's *possible* he hit *Muttle* and broke his lens," Jake agreed. "That's a really good theory, and explains why only one lens was smashed. The timing would be highly coincidental, but it does explain why nobody answered when I got there, and why the lights were off. Plus, I noticed the doctor's knuckles were roughed up.

"But he couldn't have *killed* him because Rose told me *Muttle* came to bed later that night."

Pinky put up his *stop* hand one more time. "Whoa! Since when do you take everyone at their word Sherlock? What if Rose lied about that? Or, what if she found out that *Muttle* was photographing women in the *mikvah*, and *she* killed him? *She* had access to the *mikvah*."

Chapter Thirteen

Jake invited Rabbi Miklin to dinner Monday at the Skokie *Shalomski's* on Dempster for an update.

Jake arrived first, and was escorted to his regular table at the back of the kosher-polish cuisine establishment facing front to take in all the goings-on.

An unfamiliar, young, chipper waitress bearing a *Naomi* name tag arrived to take his drink order.

"Do you want your usual drink?" she asked.

"Yes please," Jake responded reflexively with a smile, then wondered how she knew what his *usual* was.

He checked the time on his phone noting it was still early.

He heard clanking pots, and a woman barking orders *Yiddish* from the kitchen behind him.

A bit later Naomi delivered his chilled compote. She fished a straw from her apron, and handed it to Jake. "Enjoy!" she said.

Jake peeled back the top of the straw's paper cover, then carefully slid it off in one piece. He ran his pinched thumb and forefinger from the bottom to the top to flatten it, rolled it up neatly, and placed it beside the compote. He plunged the straw deep into the sugary, dried-fruit refreshment, and began his ritual of slowly nursing it.

A few minutes later he spotted the rabbi at the door, and waved him over to his table.

"I'm eager to hear your report," Rabbi Miklin said while sliding into the burgundy, leather bench seat across from Jake.

"Let's order first, then I'll fill you in," Jake said.

While they perused the menu Jake felt a hand rest on his shoulder. He turned to see Marvin Fox's warm smile. Marvin founded the Shalomski chain, and became good friends with Jake after he solved an old case involving Marvin's family.

Marvin nodded a greeting to Rabbi Miklin, then asked Jake, "So, what did you think?"

"About what?" Jake asked.

"Naomi, your waitress. She's new. Today's her first day," Marvin explained.

"Really? She seemed like she'd been working here for a while. She even knew my *usual* drink order," Jake said.

"A little trick," Marvin admitted. "I purposely sent her to your table, and told her you usually order compote. She's my oldest granddaughter. I'm taking more of a back seat these days, letting my kids and grandkids slowly take the reins managing the business. I spend most of my time popping in to each location to check in, and greet the regulars."

"Good for you Marvin," Jake said. "You've done an amazing job building the business. It's great that you have this to hand down to your kids."

Jake was genuinely happy for Marvin but felt the deep hole in his heart, having lost his only child.

After Marvin excused himself to make his rounds, Rabbi Miklin said, "*Nu*? What've you found out?"

Jake recounted how he found Dr. Eisenstein's glasses at *Muttle's*. "He's certain it's his own daughter in the picture, and that it was taken at the *mikvah*, most likely from the ceiling."

"This is terrible," the rabbi said while massaging his forehead with his fingers. "Don't get me wrong—it's good that you've made progress. But if word of this gets out the consequences could be devastating to the community. The women will be afraid to go to the *mikvah*."

Jake knew that couples were forbidden to sleep together or even touch each other during and after the woman's menstruation until her flow stopped, and she spiritually cleansed herself by immersing in the *mikvah's* pool of rainwater.

"I don't think there's anything to worry about now that *Muttle's* dead. He won't be doing any of *that* anymore."

"*Muttle*? You really think--. I just don't see it," the rabbi said while slowly stroking his beard.

"I barely knew him, but I agree," Jake admitted. "But only he and Rose had access to the attic. He probably started peeping on them for his own pleasure, then got the idea to make it profitable."

"I suppose you're right," Rabbi Miklin reluctantly agreed.

Suddenly the rabbi gasped, "You don't think Dr. Eisenstein had anything to do with *Muttle's death*, do you?"

Chapter Fourteen

The next morning Jake parked on the residential side of the *mikvah* building. He adjusted his sunglasses, zipped up his leather jacket, and pulled up the collar as he approached Rose's door.

He pressed the doorbell, and rapped on the little window in the door. He repeated the process several times before deciding to leave.

He turned back toward the car.

His eye caught a familiar figure relaxing on his webbed chair outside the KFC drive through.

Jake approached the odd man from behind. "Hi Harold!"

Harold twisted around. "Oh, hi Jake!" he replied.

"Back at your post I see," Jake said.

"Yup. What brings *you* here?" Harold asked.

"I stopped by to ask Rose Katz a few questions, but it seems she's not home."

"Oh—she's probably on the *mikvah* side waiting outside the door. Now that *Muttle's* gone she works both shifts. But she can't go in while men are still in there—*you know*. She waits for the last man to come out, and tell her it's all clear."

Jake rounded the building, and found Rose standing outside the *mikvah* door swaying while hugging a red shawl.

As he approached her the metal door of the *mikvah* scraped open. A familiar face emerged, and gave Rose a *thumbs up*.

"Hi Benny," Jake said, waving one hand. He turned toward Rose. "Do you have a few minutes?" he asked. "I have a few more questions."

"Sure," Rose said. "I need to clean up, but I can talk while I clean."

She held the door open, and motioned Jake inside. Again, he found it odd that she locked the door leaving them alone.

Rose picked wet towels off the locker room benches, and tossed them into the laundry bin.

"I'll get to the point," Jake said. "Remember those glasses on the floor near *Muttle's* workbench? Turns out they belong to Dr. Eisenstein. Do you know when he was here to see *Muttle*?"

"*I* never saw him here," Rose replied, "I was usually away during the day shopping, and running errands while *Muttle* worked. He coulda been here anytime."

Jake followed her as she wheeled the squeaky laundry bin to a large washer inside a small utility room near the lockers.

Watching her clean gave Jake an idea.

"How often do you clean the floor around *Muttle's* workbench?" he asked.

"Huh? What's that got to do with anything?" Rose asked.

"A lot!" Jake explained. "If you didn't see the glasses on the floor the last time you cleaned that means Dr. Eisenstein was there *after* that. So, when *was* the last time you cleaned that floor before *Muttle* died?"

Rose put a finger to her cheek, and tilted her head. "Now that you ask, I do remember cleaning that area right before I went shopping the day he died."

"Great!" Jake said. "What time was that?"

"Around three," she said.

"Excellent!" Jake replied.

"It is?" Rose asked.

"Yes--*absolutely*. That means Dr. Eisenstein was there *after* three the day *Muttle* died."

Just in case Pinky was right about Rose lying, he said matter-of-factly, "And you said the next time you saw *Muttle* was when you found him in the *mikvah*."

Rose didn't react immediately, but after a long pause she said angrily, "No! That's *not* right. I told you he came to bed later that night, and was gone when I woke in the morning."

Chapter Fifteen

Later that evening Jake entered his Evanston split-level, and traded his shoes for his cozy blue slippers. The *Torah* still laying on his dining room table to the right of the entrance reminded him to return it to the Young Israel *synagogue*. Since the faded letter had been fixed they could actively use it during services.

The only reason he hadn't returned it yet was that puzzling loose handle.

He stood over the *Torah*, and gently wiggled the top right handle. *Torah* scrolls have both ends wound around wooden rollers. Wooden roller plates are slipped over the top and bottom handles of each roller to protect the edges of the parchment.

Jake often held *Torah* scrolls with loose or wobbly roller plates—but never one with loose handles. So how was the handle on *this Torah* loose?

He passed through the dining room into the kitchen to fix himself a sandwich.

The fixer-upper's original wooden kitchen cabinets were stained dark brown, and encrusted with forty years of grease and dirt. It took him nine months to sand and repaint them white. To honor his mother's Dutch roots he fashioned wooden shoes into door and drawer handles, and hung blue gingham curtains on the sink and back door windows.

Jake tugged a fridge handle and heard the *whoosh* as it opened. The flood of light helped him scout a Ziploc sandwich bag filled with a few slices of leftover roast beef.

He opened the bag, and cautiously lifted it to his nose.

After deciding the questionable smell still passed muster, he lined two slices of rye with yellow mustard and tomato slices, slapped the roast beef on one, and completed the sandwich with the other.

He sat at the small, black laminate kitchen table shoved into the corner while his mouth wolfed it down, and his brain contemplated the wobbly handle mystery.

He washed that down with iced tea, and felt a sliver of roast beef lodged between his front teeth. He worked the tip of a toothpick between his teeth until it cracked—one end stuck in his teeth, and the other pinched between his thumb and forefinger. He continued wiggling the part stuck in his teeth until he dislodged the tiny bit of meat.

That's it!

He rushed back to the *Torah* to roll the scroll back

to the beginning to expose the right wooden roller thinking it cracked like the toothpick.

That would explain how the handle could be wobbly.

Rolling the *Torah* scroll back to the beginning is a usually two man job, but Jake managed to roll back until the right roller was exposed.

He was disappointed to find it intact.

He wiggled the loose handle to see which part of the pole moved.

It took a few tries until he finally noticed a tiny slit in the wood open and close as he wiggled the handle.

It didn't look like a crack. In fact, it looked expertly crafted—done intentionally.

This was even more puzzling.

Who would do such a thing?

What purpose could it serve?

He gently moved the handle back and forth, then began twisting it.

Eureka!

He continued twisting it until finely carved threads revealed themselves.

He couldn't fully unscrew it because the parchment was attached to the roller with cow sinew. He didn't have the patience to wait for a trained *sofer* to remove it, so he rationalized that whatever damage he was about to inflict could always be repaired.

Jake retrieved a razor knife from the upstairs bedroom-office, and slit the top sinew to release the upper part of the roller.

He finally managed to completely unscrew the handle, and revealed a cavity in the roller.

He used his flashlight app to peer deep into the opening.

It was empty.

Chapter Sixteen

On Wednesday, Jake called the bakery, and placed a pickup order for a sliced rye, then called Pinky. "I need to bounce something off you. Can we meet?"

"Sure! Pinky replied. But I'm home supervising some work. Meet me here."

His *home*.

Pinky's home was a huge mansion.

He'd spent part of his lottery winnings on an investigator to locate his kids after his ex-wife kidnapped them. They reconnected, and he grew very close with all five of them. They were now grown with kids of their own—more than twenty grandchildren at Jake's last counting.

Jake thought about the grandchildren he might have now if he'd overcome his fear of water, and jumped in to save Debra.

Jake pulled into the little parking lot outside the seven-car garage attached to Pinky's mansion.

Pinky purchased all the homes on the street, and replaced them with one mega-mansion. He made sure it had plenty of bedrooms and entertainment to keep his kids and grandchildren coming back often.

Jake parked facing the outdoor tennis court and pool, twins of the ones inside the back of the mansion.

"Hi Jake!" he heard booming from a speaker. "Come in through the garage."

Jake heard a garage door rumble, and waited for it to lift enough for him to duck underneath.

Pinky stood behind his red BMW sipping a tall glass of carrot juice. He raised the glass and asked, "Want one?"

Jake followed him into the large kitchen where Pinky asked Chef Maria to make one for Jake.

As Maria worked the loud commercial-sized juicer Jake shouted, "*So*, what's this *work* you're supervising?".

"C'mon, I'll show ya," Pinky hollered. He waved at Jake to follow him downstairs.

Pinky led him to the far end of the basement which ran the full length and width of the mansion. He opened a makeshift door revealing a set of stairs leading to a new deep sub basement.

Jake's jaw dropped when Pinky opened the door at the bottom of the stairs.

The room smelled of sawdust and glue. Workers in matching gray overalls were busy sawing, mixing things in buckets, and unpacking materials.

"What's this?", Jake asked.

"Sit," Pinky said while opening a metal folding chair, and placing it near the wall.

Jake shot him a puzzled look, but complied with the odd request.

"Close your eyes, and imagine sitting courtside at the United Center during a Bulls game," Pinky said.

"Okay, I'm there," Jake reported.

"Exactly—*yes you are*," Pinky explained.

Jake opened his eyes, and shot Pinky another puzzled look.

"I'm putting in a full size replica of the Bulls court, logo and everything," Pinky said proudly.

Jake let that sink in, then blurted, "You're wha—. Really? No *way*! Awesome!"

"I'll be able to relax courtside watching my grandkids play," Pinky said.

"Jake's carrot juice is ready," a voice boomed through the two-way speakers Pinky installed in every room throughout the mansion.

"Thanks, Maria," Pinky replied. "We'll be right up."

The two friends sipped their carrot juices on red leather overstuffed chairs in the living room. They watched exotic fish swim around the tank wrapped along the walls of the large room.

"What did you wanna talk about?" Pinky asked. "I'm all ears!"

Jake recounted the mystery of the loose handle on the *Torah*. "It musta been hollowed out to hide *something*." Jake said. "I just don't know what."

Pinky finished his carrot juice, then sat quietly looking up at the ceiling. "*Hmm.* What did the family say about it—the one who donated the *Torah*?" he asked.

"I haven't discussed it with them yet. That's my next move," Jake replied.

"What's their name?" Pinky inquired.

"Weiss," Jake said. "*Tuvia* Weiss is the grandson who donated the *Torah*."

"Oh! I *know* him." Pinky said. "You could just stop by the *Challah 'N More* bakery on Dempster. He's the owner."

"Really?" Jake replied. "I just called there to put in an order."

Jake thought for another moment, then said, "I was told his family couldn't afford to repair the *Torah*, but that bakery's gotta be a goldmine—it's always crowded. He must be making a fortune!"

"Things aren't always as they seem," Pinky responded. "He employs every single one of his children, grandchildren, and their spouses, just to support them. That's more people than he needs, or can *afford*. He barely pays the bills."

"Howda *you* know that?" Jake asked.

"Because I've loaned him money several times just to help him keep the lights on," Pinky replied.

Chapter Seventeen

Challah 'N More was Jake's go-to bakery, but he never knew who owned it.

He drove to the Dempster location after leaving Pinky's to pick up his order.

He entered the bakery, and stopped for a moment to savor the aroma of fresh-baked goods.

He stood behind a line of clamoring customers when he spotted a sliced rye on the counter with the plastic bag open letting it cool off. Assuming it was his order he held up the bag, spun it, then grabbed a white twist tie from a cup holder to seal it. He grabbed a long, narrow, brown paper bag from a stack next to the ties, and slid the sealed rye in it.

He went to toss it in the Nova before speaking with the owner, when he heard a woman ask for directions to an address in Northbrook. He turned back, and saw the short elderly woman trying to get the attention of a policeman standing in line. Nobody seemed to be helping her so Jake said, "I can look that up for you."

He put the bagged rye on the glass counter to free up his hand, and punch the details into Google Maps.

The app froze.

He closed and reopened it several times, but each time it froze.

He turned, and stepped toward the outside window thinking he might need a stronger signal.

When that didn't help, he embarrassingly returned to the counter, and informed the woman he had to restart his phone.

Jake slid the phone in his pants pocket, and waited for it to restart. He looked up at the counter where he'd left the rye to see an empty space.

"Hey!" Jake blurted out. "Who took my rye?"

He turned toward the woman and the officer. "Did either of you see who took it?" he asked.

They both shook their heads.

He reached for his phone to see if it rebooted only to find his pocket empty.

Thinking he absentmindedly slipped it into his other pocket with his wallet and keys he reached in there only to find that it too was completely empty.

After recovering from the shock, Jake realized someone must have grabbed his rye to distract him, then pickpocketed *both* of his pockets.

He was stunned. "Someone stole my rye and pickpocketed me! Who would *do* that?" he asked aloud.

Before anyone responded Jake heard a familiar snickering from behind him.

"Looking for these?" Pinky asked, holding up the loot.

Jake spun around. "*You*? What the hell--?"

"When I knew you were coming here, I raced to get here before you, and hid in the back," Pinky explained. "I figured it was a great opportunity to practice my new skills."

"Very funny," Jake said. "What new skills?"

"I've been watching YouTube videos learning how to pickpocket—just for fun, "Pinky replied. "This was my big chance to try it out. Sorry, I just couldn't resist."

While Jake retrieved his things from the prankster Pinky nodded toward the rear of the bakery, "C'mon, I'll introduce you to *Tuvia* Weiss. He's in the back office."

Jake followed Pinky behind the counter into the back. They passed hot ovens, and intoxicating aromas of fresh baked goods.

Pinky pushed open a door at the back revealing an elderly thin man with gray hair and a mustache to match.

"I got him good," Pinky announced. "*Tuvia*, this is my good buddy Jake I've been telling you about. He's got some questions about the *Torah* you donated."

Jake recounted how he found the loose handle, and discovered the hollow section in the roller. "Do you know what was hidden there?" he asked.

Tuvia's eyes widened, and his brows raised, answering Jake's question even before he said, "*None*! Didn't even know that was there."

"How did you get that *Torah*," Jake asked.

"My grandfather brought it on the ship from Europe to America," Tuvia said. "My dad told me his father said America would be exciting, and not to worry because he saved up plenty of money for them to live on. But he died in his sleep during the trip. When they arrived, and unpacked his things they didn't find any money. The only thing he brought was that *Torah*."

"What did your grandfather do for a living?" Pinky asked.

"He was a diamond trader," *Tuvia* responded.

"That's it!" Jake shouted. "*That* explains the hollow section."

"I'm not following," *Tuvia* said.

"Your grandfather said he had money, yet none was found," Jake said. "The only thing he brought was the *Torah* with the empty hollow section. What if he converted his savings into diamonds, and hid them in the *Torah*. That would have kept it hidden from thieves on-board, and could be easily converted to cash when you arrived.

"That handle was *really* loose when I got it back. I'll bet *someone* discovered the cavity, maybe even *Muttle*. After they unscrewed it, and took the diamonds it probably didn't fit as snugly as it did before."

"Don't diamonds have serial numbers we can use to trace them?" Pinky asked.

"Ya, I think you're right," Jake replied. "When I was a teenager, I worked for my cousin in the diamond trade one summer in Manhattan on 47th street. I bet he'll know how we can find those diamonds.

"*If* there even were any," *Tuvia* said.

Jake looked at Pinky while he tapped his pocket, then slipped out his phone. "Good thing it's still there! I'll try calling my cousin now."

"Hi Marty!", Jake said.

"Hey! How's my favorite cousin?" Marty replied.

Jake explained the situation, then asked, "Are there serial numbers we can use to find those diamonds?"

"Not a chance," Marty said. "Serial numbers weren't a thing until the 1970's. When *Tuvia's* grandfather woulda been on that ship there was no such thing."

"Any idea how we *could* find them?" Jake asked.

"Well, your best bet is to ask local dealers," Marty suggested. "I know a guy in Chicago—a *Sopoynik Chassid—Reuven* Grossman. You could start with him."

Chapter Eighteen

Raizy Waxman limped around the bed on Thursday, tucking in the top sheet. Her leg hurt more than usual today. She attributed that to all the stair climbing. This was her first day working as the Grossman's housekeeper.

The *Sopoynik Rebbe* arranged this job for her. She tried finding her own job, but when people saw how slowly she hobbled around they didn't want her.

The *Rebbe* discussed her situation with the Grossmans, and they assured him she'd be welcome, and could take her time with her chores. They even bought her a recliner, and a little table in the basement near the laundry room where she could rest when she felt the need.

Insinuating themselves into Jewish communities like the *Sopoynik Chassidim* by posing as a poor *Jewish* widow and her son served them well. Aside from the help these communities offered without question, it hampered the ability for the authorities to track them down.

Before choosing to pose as secular Jews who recently adopted Ultra-Orthodox traditions, she researched this type of community. She finalized her choice when learning they handled *issues* internally, and rarely involved outside authorities.

She fluffed the pillows, smoothed the quilt, then headed downstairs to rest her leg before tackling the next bedroom.

She settled into her plush recliner, felt and heard the leather rubbing as she lowered the back, then heard the springs creak as she raised the footrest. She was thankful to have this job, but never forgave Frank for putting them in this position.

Things were great when she married Frank. They weren't rich, but they were happy. They both worked—he as a factory custodian, and she as a housekeeper. They paid their bills, and got by.

After learning she was barren, Frank agreed to adopt, but she sensed he resented her for it.

After months of waiting, they adopted a two-year-old boy whose parents died in a car accident. She nurtured and loved him as her own, but Frank remained distant, and began drinking—*heavily*.

He stayed out past midnight, and came home reeking of alcohol.

It began with verbal assaults ending with Frank wearing himself out, and falling asleep. But when their son entered his teen years he began eating through the fridge faster than she could restock it. Frank's rants turned to their exploding grocery bills, and the verbal tantrums morphed into an occasional slap. Eventually, slaps escalated into punches that left welts on her torso, arms, and face.

She was thankful that her son was deep asleep by the time Frank came home. At least she could shield *him* from the abuse.

When her son reached adulthood, he became a night watchman at the mall. He usually got home shortly after Frank dozed off, so she was able to continue shielding him from the abuse.

One night Frank came home later than usual. She could smell him even before she opened the door. He was angrier than she'd ever seen him.

Between his mumbling and grumbling she gathered he'd been fired.

It was nearly time for her son to arrive.

She tried coaxing Frank upstairs to bed, but that seemed to fuel his anger. He swung wildly at her while growling obscenities and accusations.

"*Everyone* tells me what to do!" he yelled in a slurred tongue. "I'm not gonna let my *own wife* do it too!"

Frank grabbed a baseball bat, and swung at her.

She sidestepped his first attempt, but he cracked a

few ribs on his second swing.

She let out a loud wail of pain.

Frank wound up for a third swing just as her son burst through the front door. "*Ma*! What's wrong?"

He grabbed at the bat, but Frank was too quick.

This time he nailed her knee with such force she crumpled to the ground screaming in pain.

Frank turned and wound up to swing at her son's head.

"It's *your* fault you little *leech*," he said.

Her son blocked the blow with his arms, but Frank flung himself around, and hit him full-strength squarely on his ear.

She could see her son's mangled ear bleeding, and watched as he wrestled the bat away from Frank.

He beat Frank with the bat relentlessly, and with a fury she'd never seen in him.

He continued beating Frank's lifeless body until brains oozed from his skull.

She remembered how her son's fury made her feel safe *and* afraid. She instantly knew it was something she'd have to help him manage.

The first thing they needed to do was disappear. There was no telling how the police would treat her son, even with her testimony about what happened. She doubted his actions would be seen as self-defense after he had control of the bat.

That's when they started relocating every few years, and Raizy discovered the magic of Ultra-Orthodox Jewish communities.

The first time they tried it she saw how easy it was to fit in as *ba'alei teshuva*—newly religious Jews.

It was the perfect cover.

It explained why they didn't know the rules and customs, or even how to read Hebrew.

As long as they dressed and acted the part no one questioned their authenticity. The community was warm, and well-connected. Someone always invited them for *Shabbos* and holiday meals, found them housing, and helped them find income.

At first, she tried to stay hidden in one community.

But after that night something wild unleashed within her son.

His lust for non-kosher food, and women eventually threatened to blow their cover, forcing them to move, and start over.

She realized they'd eventually exhaust all the domestic Jewish communities. They needed to escape to a country where they couldn't be extradited, but that took the kind of money they just didn't have.

Just as she was drifting off in the recliner, the chirping of her cell phone startled her.

"*Hi Ma!*" her son said. "How's the new job?"

"You know," she said. "It's hard to get around, but these folks are amazing—*so* accommodating."

"Well, I got *really* good news," her son assured her. "I got something *so valuable* we can go wherever we want."

"Oh?" she replied. "*Something* valuable? What mess have you gotten into this time?"

"Don't *worry* Ma," he said. "I found some diamonds nobody even knows exists."

For the first time since that awful day Raizy was cautiously optimistic. If nobody knew about their existence nobody would come after him.

"Even so," she warned, "be careful not to draw too much attention. You'll need to sell them. My new employer, *Reuven* Grossman, is a diamond dealer. Take *one* diamond to him—*just* one. *Do not* take them all. Tell him you bought it for an engagement ring, but the girl broke it off. Tell him you need the money, and want his opinion on its value. Based on what he says we'll know the real value, and can sell them one at a time to different people."

She gave him *Reuven* Grossman's number, then said, "I'll tell him to expect your call."

Chapter Nineteen

Jake followed Google Maps directions downtown on Lake Shore Drive. He was on the fastest route despite the heavy Thursday noon traffic.

He exited the noisy road at East Monroe, and headed toward the juice bar where Pinky mysteriously wanted to meet instead of Blind Faith. Despite begging his best friend and confidant for an explanation Pinky refused to reveal the reason, fueling Jake's curiosity.

After parking the Nova, he switched Google Maps to walking mode, and hoofed it.

It took Jake a few minutes to find the place. The intense sun glaring off the metal sign made it hard to read.

He was looking for a restaurant or café, but this place was nothing more than a concession stand next to a covered cement patio with outdoor seating.

He heard the whipping wind ripple through the canvas awning.

Pinky waved at him from one of the seats, and joined Jake in line.

They ordered two large carrot juices.

When Jake turned toward the patio, Pinky tugged

his arm.

"*This* way," Pinky said. "There's something I wanna show you."

Jake followed him until they arrived at the Chicago Yacht Club.

"What—you're a sailor now?"" Jake kidded.

"Sorta," Pinky responded with a smirk. "I joined the club, but that's not what I wanna show you."

Jake followed Pinky along the cement dock picking up the stench of dead smelt until his friend stopped at the rear of a yacht Jake gauged to be about seventy feet.

Pinky motioned to the canvas flapping in the wind that covered the stern. A flock of screeching seagulls swooped over their heads. "You do the honors," he hollered, handing Jake one end of a rope.

"You bought a *yacht*?" Jake asked.

"Yup!" Pinky said. "Another reason for my kids and grandkids to visit. Give that a yank. I wanna see your reaction."

Jake tugged the rope with one hand while holding his carrot juice in the other, but the canvas didn't budge. He handed his cup to Pinky, then pulled with both hands to reveal the unexpected name—*My Hero*.

Jake threw Pinky a puzzled look.

"It's *you*, buddy. *You're* my hero," Pinky explained. "I wouldn't have money if you hadn't picked our lottery numbers with your computer. That paid for the investigator that found my kids, allowed me to build my mansion, and buy this yacht to give them reasons to visit me."

Pinky clasped his hands, and bowed while saying, "So thank you—*my hero* for making all this possible,"

Jake was dumbfounded. "I'm flattered," he said. "You didn't need to do that, but it means a lot to me."

"And now for the grand tour," Pinky said as he sprinted up the ramp, and boarded the yacht.

He put on a captain's hat, and motioned Jake to follow.

But Jake froze.

He hadn't set foot on a boat since losing Debra. He was still terrified of drowning. If not for that fear he likely would have his own grandchildren by now.

Pinky would be insulted if he didn't board. That's the last thing he wanted after receiving this amazing tribute.

Jake balanced himself with outstretched arms, and inched up the ramp. After firmly planting both feet on deck he followed Pinky around grabbing anything within reach to steady himself.

Pinky's captain's hat made him look like a thinner,

taller, and more muscular version of the skipper from Gilligan's Island.

He proudly gave Jake the grand tour.

He pointed out several bedrooms and bathrooms—or *cabins* and *heads* as Pinky so expertly called them. There was even a *head* with a Jacuzzi.

He led Jake into the gourmet kitchen—the *galley*, as Pinky corrected him.

"I saved the best for last," Pinky said.

Jake followed him into a room filled with leather recliners, a popcorn stand, and a wet bar. The chairs faced a blank wall.

"Watch this." Pinky said as he punched a button on the wall.

Two panels on the blank wall retracted exposing a huge flat screen monitor.

"I've got all the streaming apps, and tons of DVDs," Pinky boasted.

They settled into the recliners, put their feet up, and nursed their carrot juices.

Jake's phone squawked.

He wrestled it from his pants pocket. It was retired Detective Roberts returning his call.

Jake had left Roberts a message asking if he knew

when *Muttle* died. He also shared his theories that Rose could be the killer if she lied, and killed *Muttle before* nightfall, or it could be Dr. Eisenstein if *Muttle* died the next day.

"I'll have to ask about the time of death," Roberts said, "but even if he *was* killed the next day, Eisenstein didn't have the opportunity to kill him *and* get him into the *mikvah* unless he was the first to arrive at the *mikvah* in the morning, and killed him there. That woulda been risky, but then again it mighta been a heat of the moment thing.

"On the other hand, if he died at night Eisenstein could still be our killer if Rose helped him cover it up by lying. It's also possible Rose learned about *Muttle* taking those pictures. That would give *her* motive, means, *and* opportunity."

Jake gulped some carrot juice, then said, "So knowing *when* he was killed doesn't really help."

"Correct," Roberts confirmed. "But it gets murkier. Medical Examiner says *Muttle* received blunt force trauma to his forehead causing his brain to swell, but water in his lungs proves he was still breathing when he entered the water. Coulda been hit by a heavy flat object or smacked into a wall or floor. For all we know he slipped, and fell into the tiled *mikvah* wall, knocked himself unconscious, then slid into the *mikvah,* and drowned."

"Great," Jake replied. "We don't even have proof he *was* murdered."

"Oh ya," Roberts said. "One more thing. There was bruising around the eye with the smashed lens. Unclear if that happened before, or after the forehead trauma, but something small and round hit him in the eye. Something like a ball or a rock."

"Or a fist," Jake added.

Chapter Twenty

The closing time for Thursdays posted in Dr. Eisenstein's window said Five O'clock.

Jake flipped up his collar, and paced up and down Central waiting until just before that to enter. He didn't want a repeat of the doctor ushering him out prematurely to serve a customer.

When a church bell rang five times he approached the door. Dr. Eisenstein was already fumbling with the keys ready to lock up.

Jake hustled, and swung the door open before the doctor could insert the key.

"Where's the fire?" the doctor mocked.

"Oh, sorry," Jake said. "I wanted to catch you before you left."

The doctor motioned Jake to take one of the swiveling stools, and sat opposite him.

"What's so urgent?" the doctor asked.

Jake recounted what Robert's told him about the bruising around *Muttle's* eye. Leaving out the other possibilities Jake said, "He definitely was punched in the eye with a fist."

Jake caught a glimpse of the doctor squirming in his chair.

"The way I figure," Jake continued, "if someone wanted to kill him, they wouldn't just punch him in the eye. A punch in the eye more likely came from someone who wanted to *hurt* him—not kill him. Maybe from someone who was angry—*very* angry."

More squirming.

"Maybe they took it a step further," Jake said while watching the doctor's every twitch. "Maybe they grabbed something nearby—like a frying pan, smacked him in the forehead, and knocked him out. They mighta thought he was dead, and dragged him into the *mikvah* to cover it up."

More squirming joined by forehead rubbing.

Jake continued, "There's only one person I can think of that had access to the *mikvah* when no one else was around—*Muttle's* wife, Rose. But what could've made her that *angry*. Did you tell her about the pictures *Muttle* took."

"*Enough!*" the doctor cried while holding up one palm. "It *wasn't* his wife. *I* punched him."

Jackpot!

Jake sat silently to let the doctor keep spilling.

Dr. Eisenstein slowly continued, "I went there to get the *mezuzahs* like I said, but I also wanted to confront

Muttle. He insisted he knew nothing about the photograph, but who else could it be? I got so frustrated when he wouldn't admit anything. Guess my anger welled up, and I let go. Not my finest hour. That's probably when my eyeglass case slipped out of my pocket. I mostly wear contacts. I didn't notice they were missing until later that day. I had *no idea* they were at *Muttle's* until you showed up the other day.

"Rose wasn't even *home* when I was there, and I certainly *did not* tell her about the photograph. The *Rebbe* made me promise not to tell anyone—not the police, and *especially* not Rose. The women would panic, and stop going to the *mikvah*. The *Rebbe* said to let *you* handle it. But you didn't seem to be doing *anything,* so I *did*.

"This is *my* daughter," he said, poking his chest. "You don't understand what it's like—you don't have kids."

Jake held his tongue.

"I didn't wanna tell you. I knew it would look like *I* killed *Muttle*—but I didn't," the doctor insisted.

"So why tell me now?" Jake asked.

"Because I don't want you suspecting Rose," the doctor explained. "I don't think she even *knows* about the photograph. *I* was the angry person who hit *Muttle*, not *her*.

But I absolutely did *not* kill him. I admit I punched him in the eye," the doctor said while rubbing his bruised knuckles. But I did *not* hit him in the head or anything else. *Muttle* was very much alive when I left."

"Speaking of that," Jake said, "when *did* you go there?"

The doctor immediately replied, "I know *exactly* when because I went right after closing my place at five. Traffic was heavy. I got there around a quarter to six the day before *Muttle* died. Right after I hit him I heard a car pull up. I shut the lights, and told *Muttle* to keep his mouth shut or I'd hit him again."

Finally!

Now Jake understood why the place was dark, and nobody answered when went to get the *Torah*.

"Now, I'm *really* sorry I hit him, or even yelled at him," the doctor confessed.

"*Oh*? Why?" Jake asked.

"Because I'm pretty sure *Muttle* was telling the truth. He didn't know anything about it," the doctor explained.

"Why do you think that *now*?" Jake asked.

"Well," the doctor sighed, "after *Muttle* died, we all assumed there wouldn't be any more photographs. We couldn't exactly go looking for a hidden camera without tipping off Rose, and the *Rebbe* explicitly told me *not* to do that. He was even upset that I told you that photograph was *taken* at the *mikvah*. All was quiet after *Muttle* died, so even though there was probably still a hidden camera somewhere we left it alone."

"I *still* don't get it," Jake insisted. "What made you think it *wasn't Muttle?*"

"Before I get to that," the doctor continued, "you gotta promise not to tell anyone—and I mean *nobody* this next part."

"Nobody? Not even Rabbi Miklin? I'm investigating this at *his* request," Jake said.

"Correct, *not* even him," the doctor demanded. "I'm dead serious. *Promise?*"

"Promise," Jake agreed. "Let's have it. What changed?"

"This morning, I went to take the *Rebbe* to the *mikvah.* and found another envelope on his porch. He opened it, and turned white as a ghost."

"What was in it?" Jake asked.

"You absolutely *promise,* right?" the doctor asked again.

"Yes, *absolutely,*" Jake reassured him.

"There was a photograph in it like the one of my daughter, but not just *any* woman. It was the *Rebbe's* wife, the *Rebbetzin*. And this time they asked for an even bigger sum to keep it off the Internet, and demanded it be paid by this coming Monday.

"So, unless *Muttle's* ghost is doing this, *Muttle* was not the one who sent that picture, and probably had nothing to do with the first one either," the doctor concluded.

Chapter Twenty-One

Blind Faith had just opened on Friday when Jake and Pinky arrived.

They were seated at a table in the middle of the room.

Pinky slurped the last drops of carrot nectar from his tumbler. Jake loved him like a brother, but he was often unpredictable, and sometimes downright embarrassing.

Jake surveyed the sparsely filled vegetarian café, and caught a salt and pepper haired woman in a booth along the wall giving them the *stink* eye.

"Who was in the photo this time?" Pinky asked.

"Not important," Jake said, keeping *most* of his promise to Dr. Eisenstein. "The thing is, *now* we know it wasn't *Muttle*."

"Why d'ya say *that*?" Pinky asked.

"I think you need another shot of juice—he's *dead*, remember?" Jake responded.

"Ya, I know that mister *smarty pants*," Pinky said. "But why assume *Muttle* didn't take the *first* picture—the one of Dr. Eisenstein's daughter?"

"That seems highly unlikely. What're you

thinking?" Jake asked.

"Simple," Pinky said. "Actually, there's *two* possibilities. Maybe *Muttle* took the first picture for his own pleasure, but someone else found it, sent it to the doctor, and took more pictures after *Muttle* died. Or, maybe *Muttle* had an accomplice."

Pinky paused for a moment, then added, "Did they ask for money?"

Jake reconsidered his decision to tell Pinky *anything* about the secret he promised to keep. He should have known Pinky's knack for considering angles he'd missed would eke out the *whole* secret. But he rationalized that by not revealing *who* was in the second picture he'd be keeping the *essence* of his promise.

"Yes," Jake replied. "They're threatening to post it on the Internet unless they get paid before next Monday."

"*Aha!*" Pinky said, slamming his fist on the table so hard it made the flatware bounce.

Jake raised his hand-blinder to avoid catching another *stink* eye.

"So," Pinky continued, "*maybe Muttle's* accomplice got the idea to make money with the pictures, and *Muttle* refused. Maybe *that's* what got him killed."

"Wow," Jake said.

"Wow what?" Pinky replied.

"Those last few drops musta been infused with extra brain cells," Jake said.

Pinky nodded while morphing his lips into a huge grin, then said "That's not all."

Jake turned his palms up. "Let's have it," he said, "What *else* did I miss?"

"If this other person knows who these women are he's probably a member of the community."

Chapter Twenty-Two

Jake considered Pinky's theory after leaving Blind Faith.

If *Muttle's* accomplice killed him, how did he get *Muttle* into the *mikvah* without anyone seeing? The *mikvah* door is only unlocked during public hours.

Despite the *Rebbe's* wishes it was time to look in the *mikvah* attic.

Dr. Eisenstein may have been directed by the *Sopoynik Rebbe* not to involve Rose, but Jake wasn't. His directive was to solve these crimes, and he was determined not to let *anything* stand in his way.

He'd have to break his promise to the doctor, but there was no other way. He knew what would happen if the community found out about pictures being taken of women at the *mikvah*. If they stopped spiritually cleansing themselves after their monthly flow, they couldn't even *touch* their husbands, let alone satisfy their urges.

What would Mort do?

He imagined this conversation with his mentor. He missed Mort now more than ever.

Jake knew Mort would say keeping secrets was

never the answer.

He'd have to trust Rose.

Jake squashed Rose's doorbell, and zipped up his black leather jacket while waiting for a response.

He assumed the doorbell was still broken, and began rapping on the little window in the door.

He was mid-knock when Rose flung the door open wide, nearly sending him stumbling into her.

He watched the big smile on her face dissipate as if she was expecting someone else.

Rose had an *extra* sexy aura about her today.

Her long, red hair was completely uncovered draping onto the shoulders of her tight, black dress which was a little shorter than it should be.

Her red lipstick glistened.

She let Jake in, looked around outside the door, then bolted it shut.

"I wasn't expecting you," Rose admitted. "Is there news about *Muttle's* death?"

Jake noted again how he was alone with her behind closed doors.

He filled her in on the nude pictures leaving out the identity of the women, and asked her to keep it to herself.

Rose's reaction displayed just the right amount of

shock and horror, but something about it didn't sit right with Jake.

"I'd like to look in the attic to see if I can find anything to shed more light on who besides *Muttle* is involved, and hopefully even lead us to his killer," Jake explained.

After repeatedly insisting there couldn't be anything up there, she eventually led Jake into her bedroom's walk-in closet, and showed him the attic access panel.

"Is there any other way to get up there?" Jake inquired.

She assured him this was the only access, and went to fetch a stepladder.

Jake noted the bare wooden rod on one side of the closet. He assumed that was where *Muttle's* clothes used to hang. The rod on the opposite side bowed under the weight of enough tops, skirts, and dresses to fill a small boutique. A long shelf above the clothing ran the full depth of the closet. Plastic cubes stacked atop the shelf were filled with wigs, hats, and handbags. An overflowing shoe rack rested on the floor under the clothes.

When Rose returned, Jake extended the stepladder's legs, and noticed one pair of shoes he found particularly odd. Black dress shoes—*men's* dress shoes.

Jake took a step up, and slid the access panel to one side. He was surprised not to be showered with dust.

Someone had been up here—*recently*.

He hoisted himself up, and crawled toward the area above the *mikvah* while balancing his knees on the joists.

He used his flashlight app to peer between every beam and crevice.

The light flashed briefly as he guided it along one joist. He thought it looked like jewelry.

He slowly backtracked to locate the source, but all he found were a few shiny nail heads.

A few feet ahead he hit pay dirt.

A tiny, black, plastic object was perched above a vent in the ceiling.

It was hidden so well that he nearly missed it.

Remembering Mort's warning to preserve evidence, he pulled a neatly folded handkerchief from his back pocket to lift the object.

It looked like a miniature camera—the kind he'd seen in spy movies.

He carefully wrapped it in the handkerchief, stuffed it in his pants pocket, and backed out of the attic.

As Jake descended the stepladder Rose asked, "Find anything?"

Jake hesitated, wondering if he should tell her. "I thought I saw something, but it turned out to be some nails. But then I found *this*," he said, carefully extracting the wrapped camera from his pants pocket. As he slowly unwrapped the object enough to reveal it was a camera he caught a fleeting flash of surprise in her expression.

He couldn't decide if it was shock. or *panic*.

"I'll get this to the police. They have experts that can examine it for evidence."

Rose saw Jake out.

He waited by the Nova until she'd think he'd left.

He made sure no one was watching, then snuck back, and cupped his ear against the door.

Bingo!

She was on the phone talking excitedly to someone, but he couldn't make out the details.

Chapter Twenty-Three

Early Friday afternoon, Jake parked outside *Reuven* Grossman's Highland Park office. He pressed his hand against his pants pocket to make sure the ring was still there.

He originally only made the appointment to seek the diamond dealer's help locating the diamonds that may have been hidden in the *Torah*. But when he opened his underwear drawer while dressing to leave, he saw the ring box.

He couldn't propose to Mindy or even offer it as a gift.

Every time he opened that drawer, there it was—*mocking* him.

There was no point in keeping it, so he brought it along hoping to unload it.

He took the elevator to the second floor, and headed down a nicely decorated hallway noting the names of each business prominently displayed in their window.

Eventually he came to a door labeled 770.

No window—no business name.

But it *was* the suite number he was given.

He twisted the handle to open the door only to find it locked.

He looked up to locate the source of a whirring noise, and saw a security camera focus on him.

"Can I help you?" a woman's muffled voice bellowed from an unseen speaker.

"Uhhh...*ya*." he replied. "Jake Cooper here for *Reuven* Grossman."

The door buzzed, and he instinctively pushed it open only to face an imposing steel interior door. He heard the exterior door's lock *click* behind him.

He narrowly thwarted a claustrophobic attack by concentrating on the details of the door before him. It had a thick meshed wire glass window, and a transaction tray like the ones at gas stations and banks.

A bearded, short man wearing a *yarmulke*, black glasses, and a warm smile, approached the door, and asked him to produce a picture ID.

Jake slid his driver's license through the transaction tray, and watched as the man held it up, and looked back at Jake's face approvingly. He took a picture of Jake's ID with his cell phone, then buzzed the door open.

"Sorry about that," the man said, "We Gotta be extra careful."

He pressed his fingers to his chest, and said, "I'm *Reuven* Grossman. Come, let's sit."

Jake followed him into a tiny office with blackout shades on the window behind a small glass and chrome desk.

Reuven seated himself in an overstuffed white leather executive chair while offering Jake a seat across from him.

"How can I help you," *Reuven* asked.

"I'm hoping you can help me with a few things. First, I'd like to sell this engagement ring," Jake said while twisting in his seat to free the box from his pants pocket. "I bought it a long time ago to give to someone who refused it too many times. I'd like to sell it."

Reuven removed his glasses, and gently set them on the desk. He wiped the stone with a little cloth, then pulled a jeweler's loupe from his desk drawer.

He flipped the loupe open one-handed, and made several grunting sounds as he examined the large pear-shaped diamond.

"Nice!" *Reuven* said. "I'd be *very* interested. It's quite remarkable. Are you sure you don't want it?"

"Unfortunately, yes," Jake replied.

"I'll need to weigh it to make an offer. Do you mind

if I remove it from the setting?"

"Knock yourself out," Jake said. "I just want to be rid of it."

Jake watched *Reuven* meticulously spread a black cloth on the desk. He used tiny pliers to gently pull back the setting's prongs until the shimmering stone dropped onto the black cloth.

He used a plastic medicine cup to scoop up the stone, and deposited it on an electronic scale housed in a glass box. He slid the box's glass door shut. "Three point four carats," he announced.

He wrote an offer on a little notepad, and slid it over to Jake. It was slightly less than his cousin estimated he should get for it.

"If that's acceptable I can pay cash now," *Reuven* said. "But I don't deal in precious metals. You'll have to sell the setting somewhere else."

They shook on the deal.

Reuven spun his chair around blocking Jake's view while he opened a small safe, and counted out the cash. *Reuven* then placed a tiny sheet of blue diamond paper on the desk, and made a notation with a pencil in one corner. He folded the diamond into the paper forming a little packet, and slipped it into a small metal box with dozens of similar packets.

"What *else* can I help you with?" *Reuven* asked.

Jake recounted the story of the loose *Torah* handle.

"He was a diamond dealer in Europe, and told his family he had money they could live on in America. He died mid-voyage. The family never found any *money*—just the *Torah*." Jake said. "I found a hidden compartment in it, and then heard the family's story. I think he hid diamonds in that *Torah,* but never told anyone. It's empty now, and the handle is *very* loose. I bet someone discovered them, and took them to make some fast cash thinking nobody would be the wiser."

"Wow," *Reuven* said. "This is *so* odd."

"What is?" Jaked asked.

"Well...first off, you're the *second* person I met today wanting to sell an engagement stone because his proposal was rejected."

"Really? Who was it?" Jake asked.

"Benny Chinsky," *Reuven* replied.

"*Benny*?" Jake exclaimed.

"You seem surprised," *Reuven* said. "You know him?"

"Sort of," Jake replied. "I don't know him well."

"There's more," *Reuven* said. "As coincidental as

that might be, it's not the strangest part."

"*Oh*? Do tell," Jake said.

"He brought me a *loose* stone. Kinda odd if it was from an engagement ring he proposed with. But after I bought that one stone he asked if I'd be interested in buying more just like it."

Chapter Twenty-Four

This was the first *Shabbos* Jake spent with Mindy after selling the ring.

He was now fully committed to the relationship the only way she would accept it.

While helping Mindy prepare lunch in the kitchen they heard the front door rattle.

"I'll get it," Jake offered.

He was disappointed by any intrusion on his special time with Mindy, but managed a smile, and graciously said, "Oh, hi Harold! Good *Shabbos*. Great to see you. Come in."

Mindy joined them at the door. "We're just about to sit down for lunch. Please join us," she said.

The three stood behind their seats around the dining room table while Jake recited *Kiddush* over a goblet of wine.

He poured a little wine into each of their cups.

They all partook, and then gathered around the kitchen sink to ritually cleanse their hands before touching the *challah* bread.

Jake recited the blessing for bread over two large

challah loaves.

He cut three thick slices from one loaf, and dipped all three into a tiny pile of salt. He bit into one, and then passed one to Mindy, and one to Harold.

Mindy served two of Jake's favorites for the main course—a hot dog *cholent,* and potato *kugel.*

Jake cleared the table with Mindy wondering if he should deliver the little speech he prepared with Harold present.

When they returned to the table he went for it.

"This week I sold the ring that caused so much turmoil in our relationship," Jake said to Mindy. "I'm completely committed to live our life together the way you feel most comfortable."

Mindy stared at him briefly, then ran to her bedroom, and slammed the door.

Jake and Harold exchanged dumbfounded looks.

Jake wondered what his transgression was *this* time.

He slowly slid his chair back, hung his head, and plodded toward her bedroom. After several minutes of gentle knocking Mindy opened the door.

"Sorry," she said, dabbing her tears with a tissue. "I didn't want Harold to see me like this. Don't worry—these are good tears. I never completely believed you were okay with things even though you *said* you were. But now—*now* I know you *really* do mean it."

Jake held her tight, and kissed her forehead. "I get it," he said. "You have nothing to worry about. I don't even know *why* I waited so long to get rid of it."

He held her hand, and led her back to the table.

"All's good," he announced to Harold.

They silently enjoyed another one of Mindy's fruit tarts for dessert until Jake said, "A funny—no, an *odd* thing happened when I went to sell the ring. Benny Chinsky was there earlier that same day selling a diamond *he* supposedly bought for an engagement ring. *And* he inferred he might have more to sell. Strange right?"

Jake didn't want to say what he *really* thought in front of Harold. He could share that with Mindy later.

Harold unexpectedly raised his hand, "Oh! I know who that was intended for."

"What *what* was intended for?" Jake asked.

"Benny's engagement ring," Harold replied.

Mindy and Jake exchanged quizzical glances. Jake extended an open palm toward Harold, "*So*? *Who* was Benny proposing to?"

"Rose Katz," Harold replied.

Chapter Twenty-Five

Jake stepped out of his hot Sunday morning shower.

He faced the steam-fogged mirror, and dried his hair with a fluffy red towel.

He wiped the mirror, and was checking his wavy, dark-blond hair for new gray strands when his phone chirped.

"Morning Jake." a voice said.

He immediately recognized it as the deep authoritative voice of retired Detective Roberts.

"*Is it*?" Jake replied. "Any *news* for me?"

"Well, *that's* a fine *how-d'ya-do*," Roberts snapped.

"Sorry," Jake said, then slowly dragged out, "So, *how are you*?"

"Just dandy," Roberts snapped. "You?"

"I can't stop thinking about the two cases. I'm sure they're related," Jake said. "I just can't seem to put it all together."

Jake recounted how he learned that Rose may have rejected a marriage proposal from Benny Chinsky. Harold saw Benny drive through the KFC next to the *mikvah* building, and then go to Rose's front door. Harold thought they seemed overly *friendly* before she let him in, and closed the door.

"Benny sold a diamond to *Reuven* Grossman he *said* was for an engagement ring , then asked if he'd be interested in buying more like that one. Harold's revelation connected the dots. I think *Muttle* found the diamonds in the hidden compartment in the *Torah*, and after he died Rose gave them to Benny to sell."

"*Hmm...*ya might be onto something there," Roberts said. "Oh--I have news for *you* too. *Two* things. The forensics guys gave that camera you found the once-over. Prints on the plastic housing match prints from an open murder case in Cleveland."

"*Really*? Wow!" Jake replied. "Whose are they?"

"No way to tell," Roberts said. "No match in the system."

"You said there were two things," Jake replied. "What's the second?"

"Turns out that camera wasn't just taking stills, it was recording video and sound," Roberts said. "Some geek at forensics tracked down some sorta *sky* account in *Muttle's* name."

"*Sky* account?" Jake asked. "Was it maybe a *cloud* account?"

"Ya—cloud, sky, *whatever*," Roberts replied. "Point is, what they heard on the audio. It mostly picked up sound from the *mikvah,* but occasionally they heard a woman yelling—sounded like it came from the residence. Musta carried through the vents when her voice got loud enough. They assume it was Rose because it was between *mikvah* hours."

"Okay," Jake said impatiently. "So, *what* did she yell about?"

"She was chewing someone out for not keeping the diamonds to buy her a new kitchen, and argued that nobody was even *looking* for them. Most likely she was yelling at *Muttle.*"

"*Wow!*" Jake responded as his mind raced.

"There's more," Roberts added. "Later that same day they heard a woman—again, presumably Rose, scream."

"I don't follow," Jake said. "You already said she was yelling."

"Not *yelling,*" Roberts corrected, "*screaming.* Like a terrifying scream. No words, just a blood-curdling scream, and then silence."

Chapter Twenty-Six

Jake finished drying off, dressed, and jumped in the Nova to meet Pinky for brunch at Blind Faith Café.

Pinky was waiting for him outside the door tapping one foot while checking his watch.

"They're *supposed* to open at ten, but the door's locked," Pinky moaned. "I'm *famished!*"

"Hang in there," Jake said. "I know you'll survive. It's only a few minutes past."

Jake distracted his starving friend with the recent revelations, and how he thought the pieces fit together.

"Mort taught me that a good hypothesis fits like a glove," Jake said. "I think I'm close, but there's things that still bug me."

"Like what?" Pinky asked.

Before he could respond the door swung open.

"See," Jake said, "you're still alive!"

The moment they were seated Pinky ordered a large carrot juice while contemplating what to eat.

When his juice arrived, Jake ordered a goat cheese omelet, and Pinky opted for vegetable quiche.

"So, what's bugging you Sherlock?" Pink asked.

"Coupla things," Jake replied. "First off, I never saw Rose shed a tear for *Muttle*. She did act as expected when I first met her when she showed me *Muttle's* body. But there was something a little too perfect about that. Like she rehearsed it. After that, she didn't even seem sad—acted more *matter-of-factly* about it."

"Maybe she's just good at hiding her feelings, and keeping her composure," Pinky suggested.

"Maybe," Jake conceded.

"What else ya got?" Pinky coaxed.

"Well, Rose dresses pretty provocatively for an Ultra-Orthodox woman," Jake said. "She's got quite the figure, and knows how to flaunt it. Got my juices going more than once."

"*Ohhh-kay!*" Pinky said, leaning forward, "I'm all ears—*do tell.*"

"Besides *dressing* sexy she has a habit of being alone with men behind closed doors—a big *no-no*," Jake explained. "She did it with me, and according to Harold she did that with Benny too."

Jake paused, then added, "Plus, the last time I went there she seemed disappointed to see me when she opened the door. I think she was expecting someone else."

"*Benny*," Pinky concluded. "She probably expected

to see Benny."

"Spot on," Jake said. "The first few fingers of the glove are starting to fit. But how does all this tie into the camera, and *Muttle's* death? We're not quite there yet."

When their food arrived the two masterminds silently ripped into their dishes barely taking the time to savor their culinary delights.

Jake swallowed his last bite of omelet, leaned back, and patted his tummy. "Totally refueled. You?"

Pinky held up an index finger while he washed down the last morsel of quiche with a swig of carrot juice. "I'm there," he said.

"I keep thinking about that loose *Torah* handle, and the diamonds that musta been there for decades," Jake said. "Roberts said the camera recorded audio of a woman they assume was Rose yelling about keeping the diamonds to sell, and later she screamed. She was probably yelling at *Muttle*. Until Roberts told me that I wasn't even sure there *were* any diamonds. It was just a *theory*. But now there's some actual evidence of it.

"*Muttle* seemed like a straight shooter to me. He'd never agree to keep the diamonds. He'd wanna get them back to their rightful owner. Maybe *Rose* killed *Muttle* to get those diamonds. Maybe *that's* why she didn't seem upset he was dead," Jake surmised.

"But *Rose* wasn't selling the diamonds," Pinky pointed out. "*Benny* was. It doesn't make sense. If Rose blew off his marriage proposal he probably wouldn't be helping her."

"You'd be right, except for one thing," Jake said.

"Oh? What?" Pinky responded.

"I don't think Benny proposed to anyone," Jake said. "I think that was a ruse to see if he could sell one to establish a price. He threw out a feeler to see if *Reuven* Grossman would buy the whole lot. I think Rose was having an *affair* with Benny. I think she killed *Muttle* and asked Benny to unload the diamonds for her to avoid connecting them to her."

"So, what was the scream all about?" Pinky asked.

"Huh?" Jake responded, cocking his head to one side.

"Roberts told you there was yelling, and later a *scream*," Pinky said. "What would she have been *screaming* about?"

"*Hmm.* Maybe Rose screamed when she killed *Muttle*," Jake said. "Or maybe she screamed when she saw someone *else* kill him?

"Rose is most likely the killer—she had access to

the *mikvah* between hours. Maybe she hit *Muttle* in the head in the residence while fighting over the diamonds, then dragged him to the *mikvah*."

"*And* besides access she had more than one motive," Pinky offered.

"How so?" Jake asked.

"She mighta killed him for the diamonds," Pinky replied. "But she also mighta killed him for love. Maybe her relationship with Benny was getting serious, and *Muttle* refused to give her a *Get*. Without her Jewish divorce she couldn't marry Benny. Her only other way out would be to kill *Muttle*."

"Ya! Good thinking!" Jake said, "But that doesn't explain who sent that naked photo *after Muttle* died.

"And Roberts said there were fingerprints on the camera matching ones from another murder scene. They couldn't match it to a name, but what does that mean? Did Rose kill someone else before *Muttle*? Did *Muttle* put the camera up there, and he killed someone?"

"You said *Muttle* didn't seem the type to take those pictures," Pinky reminded him.

"I *did* say that," Jake admitted. "But forensics traced the camera to a cloud account in *Muttle's* name."

"*Even so,*" Pinky advised, "anyone could fake an

account using his name."

"Okay." Jake replied. "Suppose you're right—it wasn't *Muttle*. Who *else* had access to the attic that would take naked pictures of women at the *mikvah*?"

A split second later they each pointed an index finger at the other, and blurted, "*Benny*!"

"*Benny* coulda accessed the attic while *visiting* Rose," Jake added. "And if *he* was taking the pictures *that* explains how one turned up at the *Rebbe's* home *after Muttle* died. He musta used *Muttle's* name to open the account, like you said."

"Didn't you say Benny runs a security business?" Pinky asked.

"Ya," Jake replied. "Harold saw him driving around in a blue van—some kinda security business."

"Okay then," Pinky said. "He's gotta be pretty tech savvy. He must know all about tiny cameras!"

"Very good!" Jake said while applauding, catching rude looks from their fellow diners. "Rose had to know Benny put that camera up there. *That's* probably who she called right after I found it. She musta called him to warn him."

"*Alright*! Pinky said. "And *that* means the prints matching those at another murder scene were *Benny's*."

"*Yes!*" Jake agreed.

"*And...,*" Pinky said, nodding at Jake as if to prod him on to the next logical conclusion.

"And what?" Jake asked.

"*Oy*! C'mon! Pinky responded. "You need more carrot juice!"

"No really, *what*? I don't see it," Jake pleaded.

"If Benny killed once before...," Pinky said slowly.

"Maybe he did it again," Jake finally concluded. "*He* musta killed *Muttle!* Maybe to marry Rose, or maybe *Muttle* found out about the camera, and threatened to tell."

"Or maybe," Pinky added, "Rose told Benny about the diamonds, and he killed *Muttle* to stop him from telling anyone about them."

"And *that's* why Benny was the one trying to sell the diamonds—*for Rose!*" Jake added.

"*For* Rose, or maybe as her partner," Pinky pointed out.

"Yes! That glove *really* fits snugly now—all five fingers," Jake said. "But we need proof. I'll have to confront Rose, and see what shakes out."

Chapter Twenty-Seven

Rose shoved Benny out of her front door, and slammed it shut, causing the little window pane to rattle.

Bastard!

When Benny arrived on Sunday morning her heart raced anticipating the words she'd waited so long to hear. But that all changed when she checked his coat pockets while he showered after they quenched their carnal thirsts.

It started innocently the first day he knocked on her door when *Muttle* was away. He pitched his security services for their residence and the *mikvah*. Something about him stirred her—a tingle where there hadn't been one in a very long time.

As a good *Sopoynik Chassid* she sheepishly did as she was told. So, when the *Rebbe* selected a match *for* her she went with it.

She only met *Muttle* seven times before they married. Each *date* consisted of chatting in the *Sopoynik Rebbe's* living room while he and the *Rebbetzin* kept watch.

Muttle seemed pleasant enough. She could find no reason to reject him—until it was too late.

When their wedding night arrived, she expected to

finally satisfy her urges. She was a passionate creature that desperately needed to give herself fully to a man who would take her in every way.

But her disappointment couldn't have run deeper.

She kissed him once, passionately.

No response.

She slowly disrobed, watching intently but saw nothing stir.

She took his hands, and guided them to the right places.

Still nothing.

She seductively entertained his manhood.

Eventually she aroused him enough to penetrate her, but had to guide him every step of the way.

He silently performed his duty, and withdrew without a single moan.

The horror of her situation gripped her.

She focused on their *mikvah* duties—a gift from the *Rebbe* and *Rebbetzin* so they could make a living.

She dressed provocatively hoping to spark something resembling a man in *Muttle*.

Eventually, she realized it was hopeless.

She desperately tried to satisfy herself, but no matter what she tried she couldn't fully release the fire within.

She contemplated asking for a divorce, but loathed the way the community treated divorcees.

Her only option seemed to be to find a secret lover.

She dressed in form-fitting clothes to draw attention to her sensuous body.

She closed doors to be alone with men when she shouldn't, hoping they'd take notice of her, and act on it.

But none of them crossed the line—*until* she met Benny.

Despite his religious garb and mangled ear she sensed a manly beast within him.

So, when Benny handed her his brochure and card she made sure to *accidentally* grace his hand with hers, flesh on flesh.

She felt the spark, and watched the flash of fire dance in his eyes.

That was the moment she knew she'd snagged him.

At first, their relationship was purely physical.

But things progressed.

She developed feelings, and sensed he had too.

Their *arrangement* didn't fully mature until *Muttle* died.

She let her feelings run wild.

She dropped hints, and sent signals, but Benny didn't budge until she came right out and said those three frightful words.

She was relieved to hear them back.

She steered their conversations toward making their relationship official, but Benny insisted she wait the full year of mourning to avoid suspicion.

But she *couldn't* wait.

She convinced him they should use the diamonds to disappear, and start fresh overseas.

When Benny called to say he sold a diamond *and* had news to share she was certain he was ready to whisk her away.

They spent the entire morning in a bed of passion. It was past noon when the fire subsided.

Benny hadn't mentioned anything yet so while he showered Rose rifled through his pockets looking for tickets.

She was thrilled to find a printed itinerary.

She skimmed it, and saw they were heading to Hong Kong. But the names of the travelers listed Benny's name and his mother's name—Raizy Waxman.

Benny emerged wrapped in a black, terrycloth robe drying his hair with the hood.

She waved the printout in his face. *"What's this?"* she asked. "Your *mother* is coming with us? Where's *my* ticket?"

His silence was his answer.

There *was* no ticket for her.

Benny was leaving with his mother, and abandoning her.

He tried to explain, but she didn't want to hear it.

Finally he just said, "I only sold one diamond—enough to buy the tickets.

He reached deep into the pocket of his pants draped over a chair. "Here's your half," he said, handing her a wad of cash, and a little black velvet pouch.

After slamming the door behind him the pit in Rose's stomach grew so intense that she ran to the toilet, doubled over, and heaved.

She felt the burn of the hot mess rush up her throat, and spew into the bowl.

Before the stench dissipated a second wave ejected.

She stayed there kneeling over the toilet until she composed herself enough to towel off her blouse and face.

She cupped her hand under the sink, rinsed twice, and then gargled.

She felt her body switch modes.

Her heart began pounding so hard she could feel each pulse in her ears.

Her breathing became rapid and shallow.

The betrayal evoked a rage she'd never felt before.

There was a knock at the door.

Chapter Twenty-Eight

Jake pulled up the driveway to park outside Rose's door, nearly colliding with a blue van spitting gravel as it sped away.

Before he could knuckle the door a second time it swung open forcefully, and bounced off the interior wall.

Before they made eye contact Rose growled, "*Now what*?"

Her red-hot complexion matched her tone.

Jake fired back, "Well, *hello* to you too!"

"Oh, sorry," Rose said.

"Can I come in?" Jake asked. "I have a few more questions."

Rose held the door open with one hand, and extended the other motioning to Jake to enter.

Jake decided to leverage her mood by striking hard and fast in the hopes she'd reveal more than she otherwise would.

"Are you seeing Benny Chinsky romantically?" he asked, firing the first shot.

"*What*? No!", she replied. "Not *anymore*!"

"Oh? But you *were* seeing him." Jake said. "What

happened?

"Did *he* put the camera in the attic?

"Does *he* have the diamonds?

"Did *he* kill *Muttle*?"

Rose returned a fiery stare, then said, "I shouldn't be telling you any of this, but after what he just did to me he deserves what he gets."

She collapsed into an overstuffed, brown chair directly behind her, and said, "You better sit down. It's a long story."

Chapter Twenty-Nine

Jake lowered himself onto the worn, upholstered, beige couch next to Rose. "I'm all ears."

"I don't even know where to *start*," she said.

"When did you start seeing Benny?" Jake asked to get things rolling.

Rose took a deep breath, then blew it out slowly.

"Benny knocked on my door a few months ago. The *Sopoynik Rebbe* told him we might be interested in a security system for our home and the *mikvah*. You have to understand, I married *Muttle* because the *Rebbe* told me to. But after the wedding I quickly realized we weren't a good match. *Muttle* was a nice enough guy. He didn't earn much, but between his *sofer* business, the free housing, and the small salaries we got from taking care of the *mikvah*, we made ends meet.

"But I wanted *more*—I'll admit it. So I pushed *Muttle* to make extra money when he could. I really wanted a new kitchen.

"But it wasn't *just* about money. *Muttle* and I just weren't--. We didn't--. Let's just say I'm a *passionate* person, and *Muttle*—he was more like a dead fish. I needed more. So I looked for an opportunity.

"The moment I met Benny I felt electricity between us. Things sorta progressed from there."

"What about the camera in the attic?" Jake asked.

"As I said," Rose explained. "I wanted things we just couldn't afford. Benny came up with the idea. He said if I helped him, we could split the profits. I let him put the camera in the attic. He said he was gonna stream video of the women on a membership website. Nobody would know who the women were—nobody would get hurt. It seemed like a good idea.

"But he didn't make much money at all. He barely got enough subscribers to cover the cost of running the site.

"Nobody would get hurt?" Jake asked. "Really? What about the naked pictures of Dr. Eisenstein's daughter, and the *Rebbetzin?*"

Jake realized in his zealousness he revealed something he'd promised to keep secret.

Too late now.

"*What!*" Rose replied. "Whadya mean?"

"They were threatened to have those posted publicly if they didn't pay up," Jake said.

"I *swear*—I didn't know about that," she said. "Benny musta done that without cutting me in."

"And the diamonds?" Jake asked. "How did Benny get those diamonds?"

Rose shook her head.

"I just couldn't let it go," she admitted. "*Muttle* found them in a hidden compartment in that *Torah* you brought him. It seemed obvious that nobody knew they were there. It would have been so easy to just take them, and sell them. That could have been a real windfall for us. But *Muttle* wouldn't hear of it. He wanted to tell you about them.

"How did *you* find out about the diamonds?" she asked. "Did *Muttle* tell you?"

"No," Jake said. "Benny tried to sell them to a dealer I know. But how did *Benny* get them? And what *really* happened to *Muttle*? He didn't *accidentally* fall into the *mikvah, did he*?"

Jake could see the anger return to Rose's face.

"After what that *bastard* did to me..." she muttered.

Rose turned her head to one side as if pondering what to say next. "He deserves everything he's gonna get."

"What *bastard*?" Jake asked. "*Benny*?"

"Yes! *Benny*," Rose said. "I told him about the diamonds. We were gonna get them when *Muttle* wasn't home. Benny said we could probably get enough for them

170

to run away together. I got suckered in, and he *knew* it. *Bastard*! How could I be so *stupid*?" she said, spitting the last word.

"So, what happened to *Muttle*?" Jake asked.

"I told *Muttle* to go buy some groceries. Benny was supposed to wait for him to leave, and then come get the diamonds," Rose said. "But Benny had no patience. He arrived before *Muttle* left, and said he was here to check our alarm system.

"*Muttle* excused himself to the bathroom before leaving, so Benny rummaged through his workbench. He found the black pouch with the diamonds just as *Muttle* got back to the room.

"*Muttle* confronted him.

"Benny grabbed him by the throat, and pinned him against the wall.

"I grabbed an iron skillet, and threatened Benny to stop. But he wrestled it from me, and smacked *Muttle's* forehead.

"*Muttle* slumped to the floor. We *thought* he was dead," she explained.

"So, how'd he end up in the *mikvah*?" Jake asked.

"Benny said it needed to look like an accident," she explained. "So, we posed him in the *mikvah* to look like he hit his head, fell in, and drowned."

Jake shook his head in disbelief. "If you fell so hard for Benny, and were gonna run away with him, *why* are you telling me all this?"

Rose's eyes bulged as she stared at Jake, and growled, "Because the *rat bastard* duped me. He only sold *one* diamond. He never intended to run away with *me*. He's got a flight to Hong Kong, but not for *me* and him—they're for him and his *mother*!

"Turns out he's not only a liar but he's a real *mama's* boy to boot!"

"When's his flight?" Jake asked.

"In two days," Rose said.

Chapter Thirty

"You think she'll testify against Benny?" Pinky asked late Sunday afternoon.

The two old friends sat in the lower level of Jake's split-level home on matching black, leather reclining couches wearing their cozy slippers. The couches formed an L-shape forcing them each to nestle into the far end of their respective couches so they could both raise their footrests.

"Yup," Jake assured him, curling his toes in his slippers. "First off, she's *really pissed* at him. Second, she'll do it to save her own neck. The D.A. said they won't go after her for covering up the murder, moving the body, and filing a false report if she testifies.

"But there is one big problem," Jake added.

Pinky shielded his eyes from the sun glaring through the half-closed, aluminum blinds above Jake's couch on the back wall. "What's the problem?" he asked.

"They can't find him," Jake explained. "Benny and his mom skipped after he left Rose. The landlord has no idea where they went. Neither does the *Sopoynik Rebbe*—I called him myself."

"Didn't you say they had tickets to Hong Kong?" Pinky asked. "Can't the detectives find the flight they're on, and get him at the gate?"

"That's what *I* asked, Jake said. "They *did* find the flight. Problem is they canceled the tickets. They're probably still gonna run, but there's no telling where to, or how. *I* think it'll be soon so we need to find Benny fast. Roberts says there's a warrant for his arrest, but no manpower to search for him. But if *we* can locate him they'll definitely pick him up."

"*We, kemosabe*?" Pinky asked, holding his empty juice glass high.

"Okay," Jake said.

He heard the springs creak as he lowered his footrest to get up.

He grabbed Pinky's empty glass, and said, "Hold that thought."

Jake strode across the beige, Berber carpet, climbed the short staircase, and went to the kitchen. He pulled a large bag of carrots from the fridge, and ran them through the high-end juicer he bought specifically to satisfy Pinky's unquenchable thirst for carrot juice.

Jake could barely hear his own thoughts over the juicer's high-powered motor.

He returned with Pinky's juice. "I hope this works," he said while handing the glass to Pinky.

"Huh?" Pinky responded. "You got an idea while you were up there?"

"Funny," Jake said. "No. I hope this gets *your* juices flowing."

Pinky was already gulping it down, and didn't respond.

Jake returned to his couch, and fished around for the remote. "Let's watch TV while we think of a way to locate Benny."

He couldn't find the remote, so he asked Pinky to check *his* couch.

"You need one of those trackers," Pinky suggested. "I use them at home, and on my boat, for everything—remotes, keys, you name it."

Pinky extracted his keys from his pocket, and pointed to a tiny disc stuck on his key fob. "See," he said. "Just stick one of these babies on your remote, and use your phone to find it."

"Good idea," Jake said, then added, "*No*, that's not a *good* idea—it's a *great* idea!"

"Whaddya mean?" Pinky asked while lowering his footrest, and pushing himself upright.

"Remember when you pranked me at the bakery?" Jake asked.

"Sure. What about it?" Pinky replied.

"Can you do that backwards?" Jake asked.

"*Backwards*?" Pinky replied.

"Ya," Jake said. "Instead of taking something *out* of someone's pocket can you slip something *in* without them knowing?"

"I guess so," Pinky said. "Never tried to, but it sounds like the same basic move. How would that help?"

"Patience," Jake said, holding up one hand. "One more question first. Do you have an extra tracker doodad like that one," Jake asked pointing to the keys Pinky dropped on the couch beside him.

"Ya. I got some extras at the house," Pinky replied. "*Ohhh*...I get it. You think if I put one of these on Benny we can track him, right?"

"Bingo!" Jake said, slapping his hands on his knees.

Pinky examined his empty glass, then said, "Well, I got bad news for ya. There's two problems with your plan." Pinky made a fist and flipped his thumb up. "First, these tags are only good for about 30 feet. It's not like the spy movies."

Jake thought about that, then replied, "Okay, I

didn't know that, but suppose we *can* get one like in the spy movies. What's the second problem?"

"Think about it, genius," Pinky said. "To put a tracker in Benny's pocket we need to…" They finished that sentence in unison, "*know where he is!*"

"I think we can solve *both* of those problems," Jake said. "The police must have those kinda spy trackers. Roberts can probably pull some strings, and get us one. To put one on Benny we just need to lure him out of hiding."

"And howdya suggest we do that?" Pinky asked.

"*I* don't—*kemosabe, you* do!" Jake announced. "You're gonna kill two birds with one stone."

"I don't like where this is going," Pinky moaned.

"Hear me out," Jake pleaded. "Rose said Benny only sold *one* diamond. For the right cash price I bet he'd jump at the chance to sell them all. He knows what *Reuven* Grossman paid for one. Offering double that for the rest oughta do the trick. I'd make the offer myself, but I don't think he'll go for it. He knows I'm investigating *Muttle's* death. He'll suspect a trap. But there's an even bigger reason."

"What's that?" Pinky asked.

"I don't flaunt my money. Most people have no idea I'm wealthy. He'd never believe I could pay that kinda cash. We need someone the community knows is wealthy," Jake said peering over imaginary reading glasses at Pinky.

"Who's that?" Pinky asked.

Jake's mouth hung open while he cocked one eye, as if beaming the obvious answer to Pinky, "Seriously?"

"*Oh...*" Pinky said. "You mean *me.*"

"Yes *you!*" Jake said. "Everyone sees your mansion and the cars. And now you even have a *yacht*! Benny won't question *your* ability to pay."

Pinky rubbed his forehead, tilted his near-empty carrot juice, and caught the single drop that trickled out.

"If we can lure him out we don't need to put a tracker on him. Can't we just tell the police where to be?" Pinky asked.

"The police won't come out until we know for sure where he is. If we wait until he shows to call them, he could be long gone by the time they arrive," Jake replied.

"Makes sense. But *why* would I wanna pay double?" Pinky asked. "I don't care about the money, but why would Benny *believe* I *want* to pay double?"

"That's the beauty of it," Jake said. "Tell Benny they have huge sentimental value to the Weiss family. Tell him you're *Tuvia's* close friend, which is somewhat true, and you wanna buy them back as a gift.

"Benny'll believe that."

Chapter Thirty-One

Jake listened from the extension at Pinky's home. There was a long pause before Benny asked, "How do you *know* I have diamonds?"

"Reuven Grossman told me you were looking to unload them."

"*Good thinking,*" Jake silently mouthed to Pinky.

"Then you must know you're offering way more than they're worth– *what gives*?" Benny asked.

"If they're the diamonds I think they are they have sentimental value to a dear friend of mine. The money means nothing to me, but getting those diamonds back for him means everything."

After another long pause Benny said, "I'll need cash– and no questions asked."

"I can do that," Pinky said.

"Okay. I'll do the deal, "Benny said. "I'll meet you at Buckingham Fountain at two."

Pinky gave Jake a thumbs-up as they both clicked off their extensions.

Pinky checked his bank's Monday hours, then said, "I'll get the cash. Did you get the tracker from Roberts?"

"No," Jake replied. "They refused his request. Guess he doesn't have *unlimited* clout. But it doesn't matter."

"How so?" Pinky asked.

"Roberts says the police trackers he remembers are heavy gadgets," Jake explained. "Benny would feel that in his pocket. But I found something better."

"Oh?" Pinky responded.

"*GPS* trackers," Jake responded. "I can pick one up at Best Buy. It's tiny, light weight, *and* we can track it from an app.

"Perfect," Pinky said. "I'll get the cash while you buy the tracker. Let's meet at my yacht. It's a ten-minute walk from there to Buckingham Fountain."

Jake hesitated at the foot of the ramp leading to the deck on Pinky's yacht.

Choppy waters bobbed the ramp.

He clutched the Best Buy bag as if it would save him from drowning, and heard the metal ramp creak with each step.

The moment he set foot on board Pinky yelled, "Over here!" motioning Jake to join him on an overstuffed, white and blue couch on the deck.

As Jake approached, he noticed two tall glasses of

carrot juice on the coffee table—one already half-empty.

He planted himself on the couch, and plopped the Best Buy bag on the table letting the wind rustle through it.

"What's this?" Jake asked while patting a small blue and white, canvas duffle bag with black handles, bearing the Chicago Yacht Club logo.

"The cash," Pinky replied. "Figured I'd do this up classy instead of just handing him wads of cash."

"Nice," Jake said. "That'll make your job *much* easier."

Pinky cocked his head to one side giving Jake a puzzled look. "How so?"

"*Duh!*" Jake responded, "No need to slip the tracker in his pocket. Just hide it in the bag."

Pinky said, "*Uhhh*, you better take a swig of carrot juice, and give that more thought."

"*Why*? What's wrong with putting it in the bag?" Jake asked.

"Too risky," Pinky replied. "He's gotta be super suspicious already. He might check the bag for a tracker right away, or when he gets to his hidey-hole. The moment he ditches it and runs we're outta business—*game over*. But he's unlikely to suspect I slipped something in his *pocket*."

"Good thinking," Jake said.

Chapter Thirty-Two

Shortly before two, Pinky hiked to Buckingham Fountain from his yacht.

He saw the glorious fountain before he could hear it—the sounds of Lake Shore Drive traffic, a wailing fire engine, and a roaring motorcycle filled his ears. But as he drew closer the thundering water drowned everything else out.

The rays of sun lighting up the streams of water, the cold wind spray hitting his face, and the picturesque Chicago skyline backdrop mesmerized him.

"You got the cash?" a voice asked from behind him.

Pinky spun around to face a clean-shaven man, wearing a blue Cubs cap, and matching windbreaker.

Only the cauliflower ear gave away his identity.

Pinky raised the duffel bag in response, then asked Benny, "You got the diamonds?"

Benny tapped a bulge in his right jeans pocket. "Right here," he said.

Pinky noticed a black drawstring peeking out of Benny's pocket.

"Gimme the cash, and I'll give you the diamonds,"

Benny insisted.

"Funny," Pinky said. "You think I'm gonna *trust* you?"

"So, how're we gonna do this?" Benny asked.

Pinky instinctively thought of a solution—*and* the perfect opportunity. "We'll do the exchange at the same time. You grab this handle while I hold the bag. I'll grab that drawstring poking out of your pocket while you hold your hand over it. When I count to three, we both let go—you take the bag while I pull the diamonds out of your pocket. How's that sound?"

"I'm good with that," Benny said.

They pulled off the exchange as agreed with one exception. When Pinky slipped the diamonds from Benny's pocket, he also made a deposit.

Chapter Thirty-Three

Jake swirled the last few drops of carrot juice around the bottom of his glass just as Pinky stepped onboard.

"All set," Pinky said. He pulled a small black bag from his pants pocket, and dangled it. "I got the diamonds."

"What about the tracker?" Jake asked.

"Piece a cake," Pinky replied. "Couldn't have gone better. He has no idea."

"Awesome!" Jake said. "Now for the fun part. Let's see where that little weasel goes."

"By the way," Pinky added, "I almost didn't recognize him. He shaved his beard and *payos,* and he's wearing a Cubs cap and windbreaker."

Jake tapped the tracking app, and waited until a flashing red dot appeared. He watched the dot move for several minutes before Pinky asked, "*Nu*? Where's he headed?"

"It's the weirdest thing," Jake replied. "He's not going anywhere."

"Maybe he parked, or just stopped walking," Pinky said.

"No, he *is* moving." Jake said, "And he's definitely not on foot—he's going too fast for that. But he's not *headed* anywhere. Seems like he's randomly driving around the Loop—goes down one street, turns on the next, then heads back up again."

"That makes sense," Pinky said.

Jake looked up from the app. "It does? Looks like he's lost to me."

"Nope," Pinky explained. "He knows exactly what he's doing. He's making sure he's not being followed."

Jake raised his carrot juice glass. "I gotta start drinking *more* of this."

Jake continued following the dot until Benny finally exited the Loop off Jackson, and headed north on Lake Shore Drive.

"Now he's heading back this way," Jake announced.

He watched Benny turn onto Monroe, and follow the road.

"Damn!" Jake said.

"*Now* what?" Pinky asked.

"He's *here*—at the yacht club! How the *hell* does he know we're-- I thought he didn't know about the tracker. He must be using it to track *us*!"

"That's *impossible*!" Pinky insisted, then yelled,

"Shut your phone—quick! Power it down, *now*!"

Pinky started down the stairs below deck. "Follow me!" he commanded.

Jake followed him downstairs past the cabins all the way to the back. He watched Pinky twist a sconce on what seemed like a solid wall in the hallway. A panel retracted revealing a panic room.

He followed Pinky inside, and heard a *whoosh* as the panel closed behind him.

Pinky flipped a switch on a wall panel.

A bank of monitors came alive displaying every angle surrounding the exterior, deck, and the hallway they just left.

Jake scanned the monitors for movement.

His heart pounded.

"I don't get how he did this," Pinky mumbled. "It's *not possible*."

They watched, and waited for Benny to appear, but nothing stirred except some flags, and the water.

"Where the hell *is* he?" Pinky said. "Turn your phone back on."

Jake complied. "I see the dot. He's not moving, but he's *very* close. Why can't we see him on one of the monitors?"

Pinky rubbed his forehead with one palm. "We woulda seen him if he walked past us. He must be on one of the yachts closer to the club."

Pinky twisted Jake's hand to see the app. He zoomed in with his thumb and forefinger, then pointed to a spot on the app near the red dot. "Yup, *that's it*!" he said. "We're here, and he's on that side of us, closer to the club."

"Odd," Jake said. "If he tracked us he'd be looking for us until he found us. But he's not moving."

"I *knew* it!" Pinky blurted. "He *didn't* follow us. He *couldn't* have."

Jake gave him a puzzled look.

"He didn't *track* us here," Pinky said. "*This* was his *destination*. He must have a getaway boat docked here."

Jake called Roberts to fill him in.

"You *sorta* know where he is," Roberts said. "I'll put in a call, but until you put eyes on him, I doubt they'll send anyone."

"Roberts says we need to actually see him before the police will come get him," Jake said to Pinky.

Jake looked for a button near the panic room's entrance. "How do I get *outta* here?"

Pinky pushed a button on the control panel. The entrance *whooshed* open.

"Wait!" Pinky said. "I'll go with you."

They climbed up to the deck.

"*Lemme* see the app again," Pinky insisted.

Jake handed his phone to Pinky.

"He's two slips closer to the club," Pinky announced. "Let's go!"

They disembarked, and headed toward the club.

Jake sprinted ahead of Pinky.

Pinky stopped to tie his shoe. "Wait up," he yelled.

But Jake was too far ahead, and too fixated on putting eyes on Benny to hear him.

Jake spotted a small yacht named *Hidden Gem* docked right where Pinky showed him on the app.

He turned to tell Pinky he'd found it, but saw Pinky busy tying his shoe.

This yacht didn't have a boarding ramp, but it was much smaller, and lower than Pinky's.

Jake gauged the fluctuating distance from the dock to the deck as the choppy water rocked the vessel.

The fear of drowning gripped him just as it had when he woke to find only Debra's tiny life vest in the boat.

If he'd conquered his fear she might have lived.

He wanted to overcome his phobia, but never

learned to swim.

Jake pushed those thoughts aside to focus on the task at hand.

He gauged the timing between the tiny yacht's dips and forced himself to lean forward over the water just in time to latch onto the gleaming brass railing with his right hand in sync with the next dip.

The choppy water sent the railing upward lifting him off his feet.

He summoned the strength to pull himself up, managed to wrap his left hand around the railing, and hoist himself aboard.

He turned to find Pinky, but the next dip sent him sliding feet first under the railing.

He grasped a rope hanging from a bell on the railing to avoid falling overboard.

The loud *clang* pierced the silence.

Jake pulled himself to safety, and could now see Pinky running toward him.

"What the *hell* are you doing on my boat?" A voice barked behind him.

Jake turned to see Benny sans beard and *payos*, wearing a Cubs cap and matching windbreaker, just as Pinky described.

"It's *you*! *Dammit*!" Benny growled. "Hey Ma! We got trouble."

"*Gotchya*!" Jake declared.

"The *hell* you do," Benny replied while rushing Jake like a Chicago Bears linebacker.

Benny rammed Jake forcing him backward toward the railing.

Jake managed to keep his footing, and shoved back.

Benny crouched to ram Jake again when a gray-haired woman emerged from below deck.

She limped toward Benny waving her hands wildly. "Benny, *stop*! Not like this!"

But it was too late.

Benny lunged at Jake just as Pinky boarded.

Pinky grabbed at Benny's windbreaker to hold him back, but he missed by a hair.

Benny hit Jake like a bull, and sent him careening backward over the railing.

Jake's legs flipped up and swung back so forcefully it caused him to do a one-eighty.

His torso slapped the cold choppy water.

He thrashed around for a few seconds, and then held his breath as he slowly sank.

The cold, choppy water swallowed him.

He wondered if Debra was this terrified.

Drowning seemed like a fitting punishment for not saving her.

He couldn't hold his breath a second longer.

His lungs forced him to exhale.

He traced his air bubbles up as they rose while he sunk even further.

He wondered when he would hit bottom.

His empty lungs were about to force him to inhale when he spotted a figure diving into the water above him.

A steel arm clamped his chest from behind, and pulled him up.

The moment his lips surfaced he gasped, and felt a deep sense of relief as the air filled his lungs.

The steel arm belonged to an officer who dragged him onto a police boat, and perched him on a bench.

Retired detective Roberts draped a heavy, blue, wool rescue blanket over his shivering body. "Thought we lost you there for a second," Roberts said.

"Ya," Pinky added. "Maybe I need to put a tracker on *you*!"

Chapter Thirty-Four

On Tuesday, Rose unlocked the *mikvah* to prepare for the men.

Benny used to stand guard until she finished preparing, and made sure every man left before she went in to clean up.

But now, she was on her own.

She taped a cardboard sign to the door alerting any early birds to wait, and started her ritual.

When she was done, she removed the sign.

Later, she'd be waiting outside asking each man exiting if he was the last before entering to clean up.

She fantasized about being in there alone with them, but if even one reported her, she could be fired.

Instead of living out her *real* fantasy she had a safer way to satisfy herself.

During her marriage to *Muttle* she was forced to keep her unquenched yearnings bottled up until she discovered a way to release her urges every morning.

She needed relief *every* day, and today was no exception.

She scurried back to the residence, locked the door,

and climbed into the attic.

She confidently crawled to what *used to be* her secret spot—where Jake Cooper found the camera. He assumed *Muttle* put it there to satisfy himself, but *Muttle* wasn't even aware of that spot.

She told Benny about it. That's when he got the idea to profit from it.

But even Benny didn't know her *real* secret.

Most of the *mikvah* men repulsed her.

But *some* were worth the wait.

She reached the perfect vantage point, and waited for one of her favorites to disrobe.

Chapter Thirty-Five

Jake and Mindy waited outside the *Sopoynik Rebbe's* home for Pinky to arrive.

Jake checked the time on his phone. "He knows I hate being late," he said.

"He'll be here," Mindy replied. "Have patience. Nobody expects us to be precisely on time for a luncheon."

Jake was relieved when he heard the roar, and then saw Pinky's Lamborghini round the corner.

He anxiously waited for his friend to take his time parallel parking his precious vehicle behind his refurbished Nova.

When Pinky emerged, Jake frantically waved, and tapped the imaginary watch on his wrist.

He was about to turn, and head toward the *Rebbe's* home when the Lamborghini's passenger door flung open. The salt and pepper head of retired Detective Roberts emerged, and waved at Jake.

Pinky shot a thumb toward Roberts. "Surprise!"

"*Wow*!" Jake said to Roberts. "Didn't expect to see *you* here."

"Yup!" Roberts replied. "Got a personal invite from

the man himself." Roberts held up a *Challah 'N More* bakery box. "Even stopped to bring dessert."

The *Rebbe and Rebbetzin* greeted the four guests at the door. They exchanged greetings, and were seated at one end of an enormously long dining room table.

Their end of the plain white tablecloth was laden with a tuna noodle casserole, a fresh salad, and a large glass pitcher of iced tea. A braided *challah* rested before the *Rebbe*.

"Shall we wash?" the *Rebbe* asked.

He led everyone to the kitchen where they cleansed their hands, and recited the proper blessing while drying them.

Jake talked Roberts through the unfamiliar ceremony.

They returned to their seats, and waited silently.

Roberts started to reach for the iced tea, but Jake discreetly touched his arm motioning him to wait.

The *Rebbe* lifted the *challah,* and recited the blessing for bread. He sliced it up, and dipped the slices in salt before biting into one slice, and passing the rest around.

"Dig in everyone," the *Rebbetzin* said. "Don't be shy—we're not formal when it's just us."

She passed around the casserole and salad.

After they filled their bellies, and had ample time to chat, the *Rebbe* cleared his throat loudly while wiping his mouth with a white linen napkin.

"I want to thank the three of you," he said, nodding at Jake, Pinky, and Roberts, "for helping us root out the troublemakers disrupting our little community. You are each remarkable people. And *you* Detective Roberts—so nice to meet a real *mensch*."

"*Retired* detective," Roberts corrected. "But the *real* heroes here are Jake and Pinky. *Me?* I just lent a hand where I could."

"So, what happens now?" the *Rebbetzin* asked Roberts.

"Well, our *friend* Benny is in *real* hot water," Roberts explained. "They're charging him for *Muttle's* murder. He'll also be charged with assault, and possibly *attempted* murder for knocking Jake overboard. Then there's the matter of his—his little photography *sideline*," Roberts continued while winking at the *Rebbe*. "One way or another he's getting locked up for a *very* long time. He may also be charged with another murder. The prints found on the camera belong to Benny, and match prints found on the baseball bat used to kill his adoptive father. Raizy says Benny was trying to save her, but her word may not carry much weight. Seems she and Benny have been scamming Jewish communities like yours all over the country. They're not even Jewish. They've been on the FBI's radar for years. But they move frequently, and embed themselves in communities that won't turn their own over to the authorities. Those two were pretty clever, I'll give 'em that. They learned how Ultra-Orthodox Jewish communities openly welcome newcomers, and help support them. They leveraged that play to the hilt. And the *real* genius of it was nobody questioned their ignorance of Ultra-Orthodoxy because they posed as secular Jews who decided to become religious."

"What about Rose Katz?" the *Rebbetzin* asked.

"She'll probably get immunity if she follows through and testifies," Roberts replied.

"You know," Jake said. "I find the whole Benny and Rose thing strangely befitting."

"Oh? *How so*?" the *Rebbe* asked.

"Benny and Rose got into this mess because Benny pursued *Muttle's* wife. And the *Torah* passage *Muttle* was fixing for me is what got him killed."

"I don't follow," the *Rebbe* said.

"*Muttle* was fixing a faded letter in the tenth commandment—the part about *don't covet your neighbor's wife*."

"Amazing," the *Rebbe* said. "You really *don't* miss a thing."

"The good part is," Pinky added, "*Tuvia* Weiss got his diamonds, and now knows his grandfather didn't let them down. He really *did* save money for America. I even bought back the one Benny sold to *Reuven* Grossman."

The *Rebbetzin* turned to Jake. "I *heard* you discovered Benny had the diamonds when you sold the engagement ring you bought for Mindy."

She nodded toward the *Rebbe*.

"The *Rebbe* and I agree we made a bad *shidduch* matching Rose with *Muttle*." The *Rebbetzin* wagged a finger between Jake and Mindy as she said, "But we absolutely adore the two of *you* as a couple. You've been together so long. What's the problem Jake?"

"It's not me," Jake said while cupping his fingers to his chest. "I've proposed repeatedly."

"Well then," the *Rebbetzin* said in a chipper tone, "maybe you should just ask *one* more time."

Before Jake could respond Mindy blurted, "Yes, maybe he *should*."

*****

If you enjoyed this book and would like to read more Jake Cooper Novels, please help me by rating and reviewing this book on Amazon.com.

To receive my free bonus material* visit my website at
shop.irvsegal.com

*Includes an audiobook with pronunciations and an ebook with a glossary of the Hebrew and *Yiddish* words and phrases used in my Jake Cooper novels, and an extra "something" I think you'll enjoy reading!

*****

JAKE COOPER NOVELS BY IRV SEGAL

#1 Secrets of the Rabbi's Mafia (2023)
#2 Fatal Flaw in the Tenth Commandment (2024)
#3 Murder of a Kosher Pig (coming late 2024)

Visit shop.irvsegal.com to see the latest list of
Jake Cooper Novels

Made in the USA
Monee, IL
15 July 2025

21193104R00118